When the Third Time Was Not a Charm

Damita Cox

DAMITA COX 2020
FIRST EDITION
First Printing 2020
ISBN: 978-1-734-83913-5
Email: info@damitalynn.com

Acknowledgements

I give honor and Glory to my Savior, Jesus Christ. God will always be the head of my life. I sometimes go astray but like I have explained to people I will only go so far before God snatches me back and admonishes me to get my act together.

I would like to next acknowledge my Mom, Clarissa Smith, Dad, the late Eugene Smith Sr, Brother, Eugene Jr. and my Sister, Kristin Atkins. My Aunts and Uncles. They have always believed in me and encouraged me. I don't want to leave out my daughter Danielle Hussey and my Cousin Deborah Smyles. These two people have seen me go through so many changes in my life and never judged me.

I have the best friends in the world starting from Church, my old neighborhood and people I have met from different jobs that I have had. There are three ladies that mentored me: Karen Goodard, Robin Mitchell and Annette Challenor, they were my Managers at one point, they encouraged, trained and motivated me to be a better person. My Sister called me one day and asked me when I would be coming out with my book.

I am so glad she encouraged me to write. She never let me forget that people need to hear this story. Last but not least Joyce Black, my writing coach.

CONTENTS

Prologue

————•••••————

Who are we? Really have you ever thought about who you are? Why are you here? What is your purpose on this earth? What lessons are we learning and are we passing this knowledge on to anyone so they can prosper? The main character Destiny always knew that she was a little different than most kids. Destiny grew up around her cousins who were 3,4,5 ad 6 years older than her respectively. She was a little bit more mature than most kids her age. Some people would say she was weird. She didn't think she was weird, she thought that God created her to be different for a reason. She just didn't know why he created her to be different. Destiny wondered why God put her here on earth. She was determined to get that answer no matter what she had to go through to get it.

We are Spiritual creatures made up of Body, Soul and Spirit in Biblical teachings. The older most people get they want to explore these facets of their being. Destiny felt in order to grow she needed to embrace Godly and Spiritual teachings. After years of running from her calling, she finally gave in to God's call on her life of ministry on her life. She was licensed as a Minister then ordained. This a story of inner strength, overcoming depression, loving yourself, and finally learning to live a faith filled life.

This story is about a girl who yearned to be the best person she could be but through the years she encountered circumstances that made her question her existence. God showered his love on her and she then realized that anyone can get through various trials and tribulations in their life. This story is meant to encourage anyone that has hit some low times in their life. Destiny suffered through domestic violence and depression but found her voice and went on to live a victorious life. The devil has a mission, which is to steal, kill and destroy your life. Destiny felt she needed a relationship with God in order to navigate life.

Growing up Destiny was close to her Mom. She was the perfect Mom to her. Her Mom was intelligent and supportive. She made her want to be perfect. She was scared of her Dad, but she admired him. She thought they were the best parents in the world. A smart Mom and a talented Street-Smart Dad. She started comparing every guy she dated to her Daddy. Her brother and Dad started blocking her action way back in the day. She needed to figure out how to get away from those blockers, no wait her brother added their Cousin Leon to the mix. Oh no she thought "I will be an old maid if they have their way". She always suspected their blocking ways. When she got older Cousin Leon admitted to his dirty work. While attending High School they would threaten boys. They would tell the guys at her high school "I will throw you down the stairs if you don't stay away from Destiny." Now she knew why the guys in High School would run away from her when she spoke to them. She thought to herself is my breath kicking? She was so glad they were older, and they graduated before she did. At least she could have a couple of dates before high school ended. She was glad to have fun at school without their interference.

Destiny didn't want to be married more than once. She wanted to be like her Mother who only had one husband and all her children had one father. When her first marriage didn't last because of adultery and excessive drinking she was so disappointed. Her second marriage produced her child and she thought they would be together forever, but he was physically abusive to Destiny. Her third marriage was a dream come true, so she thought until it wasn't!

CHAPTER 1

In The Beginning

T he first child born to the Scott family was Edmond Jr. and a year later Destiny. Destiny arrived June 5, 1963 at 2:00am in the Morning. When her Mom looked at her, she said" She is destined for great things." Wow was she right with that affirmation. Her Mom like most Mom's thought Destiny was the cutest little baby she had ever seen. Her brother had beautiful brown skin with reddish tones. Courtney expected little Miss Destiny to look the same way. Why was she so very light? Her Mom had a brown complexion, she was 5'8 taller than most women, she had long black hair and she was model thin. Her Dad's complexion also had reddish tones, but he was little bit lighter than his son Edmond Jr., he was 6'2 he had a medium build and curly hair. Her Mom Courtney thought the people at the hospital switched her baby because of her light skin. Nope, she was with the right family. Her paternal grandmother, Maria Bradley was very light with soft curly sandy brown hair. Destiny inherited that same soft curly sandy brown hair. She did turn a little bit brown as time ticked on. Her skin was a beautiful caramel color with reddish under tones. She grew up to love being African American and she loved her caramel color.

Courtney's Sister was a famous Blues and Jazz Singer, Diana. She purchased a beautiful house for Courtney's Mom. Destiny's Mom and her family were living in Ida B. Wells a housing project in Chicago, Illinois. Diana moved them out when Courtney was 5 years old. Destiny's Mom grew up in a white neighborhood on the Westside of Chicago. When Destiny's parents were married, they moved into Courtney's Mom's home. Mrs. Alberta James was a dark skin, heavy set woman and she was 5'6. Alberta was also a strict religious woman who spoke her mind. She was very opinionated and didn't care how you felt about her. She only agreed to let Courtney marry Edmond if he promised to let her continue her college education and graduate. Edmond kept his promise to Alberta. It took Courtney a little while to graduate, because she became pregnant twice while attending college. Edmond worked at night as a machinist in order to provide for his growing family while Courtney attended College at Roosevelt University, located in Downtown Chicago, Illinois. Edmond kept his promise to his Mother-in-law. He knew, if he crossed Alberta by not allowing Courtney to continue her education and graduate, it would be hell to pay. Courtney was able to take care of her children and not worry about paying bills or graduating.

Edmond loved is Mother-in-law, but it was only a matter of time before they bumped heads. Alberta had turned the upstairs into several apartments. Alberta and Edmond did not see eye to eye on a situation. They had a huge argument and Edmond told Courtney that they had to move. Courtney knew that Edmond was blowing the situation out of control. She knew he just didn't want to live in his Mother-in-laws apartment. Courtney was sweet but a little stuck up. After all she was raised in an affluent family, when Edmond told her he was moving into a new housing development on the north side of Chicago called Cabrini Green, she almost fainted.

Courtney immediately called her Sister Diana. Diana had spoiled Courtney and she was used to getting her way. She begged her sister to talk some sense into Edmond, but Diana said, "I don't get mixed up in married people's business!!" Courtney was not about to give up. She had one more trick up her sleeve. Courtney knew that Diana had a soft spot in her heart for baby Destiny. She asked her sister, "Don't you care about the safety of your only niece? It's dangerous over here. We are in the projects. Diana told her sister, "I grew up in Ida B. Wells and I turned out great." She told her to give it a chance. Diana told Courtney that if things didn't work out, she would talk to Edmond. Courtney was a little happier.

Courtney decided to make sure she got her way. She decided to call her big brother Evan in Los Angeles, California. She was a very smart woman. She knew that her husband looked up to Evan. He was a judge that worked in the Juvenile Division in Los Angeles. Her brother didn't want to get involved either. Courtney was back to asking Diana. She knew Diana was stubborn but if she kept begging her. She knew she would get her way eventually. Diana usually gave in to her younger sister. After all she was so happy when Courtney had Destiny. Courtney's Sister had lost a baby girl 2 years prior. Diana had two sons; Gino and Roberto. She wanted a baby girl so bad. She loved Destiny and loved coming to see her.

She told Diana that she would come and visit them in Cabrini Green. She wasn't scared at all when she visited. She would wear her mink coat and dare someone to try and take it. She was sometimes accompanied by a personal bodyguard who was also a Chicago police officer. When he wasn't with her, she was packing a pistol and she was not afraid to use it.

Diana had to be tough to be in show business especially in the 40's 50's and 60'. Black people weren't always treated well. Many times, they had to come in through the back of the venue or through the kitchen. When she traveled. There were some hotels she couldn't stay at and if they did allow her to stay there. She might not be able to use the restaurants and pools. There was an instance where her two sons were swimming in the pool, when the boys got out the hotel drained the pool. They acted like her boys were dirty. She was furious but this was the world she lived in and there were certain things she had to put up with on a daily basis.

Diana told Courtney that when Destiny turned two years old, she was going to give her a white mink coat. Courtney told her sister, "What does a two-year-old need with a fur coat? Unfortunately, when Destiny was 6 months old her famous aunt died in her sleep at the age of 39 years old. Courtney was devastated. She was very close to her older Sister. Courtney's sister, Diana was 14 years older than her. Courtney's mother was still alive but with her sister being so much older than her it was like she was her second mother. She would travel with her famous sister when she was a teenager. When Courtney got married, she stopped traveling with her sister. Courtney vowed that Destiny would know all of her aunt's history. She told her stories about her famous aunt every chance she got. She made sure to tell her that her aunt had been married 7 times. Courtney thought this would make Destiny not want to get married more than once, after all Courtney knew she would be with Edmond until death separated them.

Courtney's sister's funeral was filled with famous people, family, media, friends and her fans. Courtney had another sister who was younger, and an older brother. Destiny's Dad had 8 other siblings. Courtney grieved over her sister for a while, but she knew that she had 2 small children to raise. The best way to honor her sister was to keep her legacy alive by singing her songs and helping those who wanted to write books and plays about her life.

Courtney finally got her way. Edmond Sr. found a beautiful newly built apartment building on the Southside of Chicago to move into. It was in a middle-class area and he knew his wife would love the two-bedroom apartment. When he told her, they were moving out of the projects. She was elated. Courtney loved her husband so much, that is why she went along with them moving out of her Mom's building even though she didn't want to. Edmond was right, Courtney loved their new apartment on 9201 S. Halsted in Chicago. It was walking distance from his oldest sister Emma.

The Scott's lived in the apartment building for 2 years. They decided it was time to purchase a raised ranch house. It was a newly built home. Courtney was super excited about her new home. It was still close to his oldest sister Emma's house. Edmond was grateful to God for blessing his family. Edmond and Courtney were both 25years old when they moved into their beautiful home. Destiny was 4 years old and Edmond Jr. was 5 years old when they moved into the new house. Destiny's parents loved their extended family. Whenever a family member needed help the Scott's were there to help them. Her Dad's younger brother Tommy fell on hard times and he lived with the family for about a year. He was a martial arts instructor and he would later show Edmond and Destiny how to defend themselves. His younger sister Gina also lived with them for 6 months when she was forced to leave her abusive husband. She was a teacher and when she felt it was safe to move, she decided to go back home to her parents because she discovered she was pregnant by her soon to be ex-husband.

Destiny was very close to her family. She knew that if she couldn't talk to her parents, she could talk to her two older cousins Mary and Margie. Mary was 6 years older than her and Margie was 4 years older than Destiny. They were the daughters of her Aunt Emma. Emma was the oldest of 9 children on her Dad's side of the family. She was Destiny's Dad's oldest sister. Aunt Emma was a very firm woman who didn't play. Destiny was afraid of Aunt Emma at first. She stood 6'0 tall in her bare feet. As a child, a woman this tall was different and scary to deal with. Yes, Destiny's Mom was tall but not that tall like Aunt Emma. Aunt Emma would not hesitate to take a switch to your backside. She respected Aunt Emma and never got one of her famous whippings. Destiny's brother Edmond Jr. was not so lucky. He received one of her whippings. Whatever he did to receive that whipping, he never did it again. In fact, Aunt Emma would snatch a loose tooth out of your mouth and would not even blink!

Destiny had a lot of respect for Aunt Emma, because she and her husband Uncle Eric were the parents of 5 children. They allowed two more children to come into their home. Destiny was a cry baby when she first started coming to their home. She missed her Mom. Her Mom had to work a lot and Destiny wasn't very understanding of her mother leaving her with her Aunt Emma or any one for that matter. The crying drove her aunt crazy. Aunt Emma asked her mother-in-law Esmeralda, who was a very evil woman what she should do about Destiny's continuous crying. Esmeralda said, "Throw that brat into a dark closet. She will stop crying. You just watch and see." Well, it did work Destiny did finally stop crying.

Destiny told her mother what happened years later that her aunt had put her in a dark closet to stop her from crying. Destiny begged Courtney not to say anything to Aunt Emma. Courtney was furious with Emma. Courtney told Destiny, "She could have scarred you for life. What the hell was she thinking?" When Destiny was growing up. She was taught not to question any adult. Which is why she never mentioned anything to her Mom regarding what Aunt Emma did to her. Destiny knew when she got older that what her aunt did was a form of abuse. She knew that her father would go crazy if he found out what his sister did. After all, Edmond was the one who thought his sister would protect his children. When Courtney told him, he was very upset. Courtney told Edmond; I will talk to Emma. Edmond agreed. He always had the utmost respect for his sister, and he knew he had a bad temper that is why he agreed to let his wife talk to Emma.

Destiny tip toed by her Mother's bedroom door so she could hear the conversation her mother was having with her aunt. Courtney had phoned Aunt Emma to ask her about what she did to Destiny. Emma was not only her sister-in-law, but she was also one of Courtney's best friends. Destiny started to feel guilty, after all if it wasn't for her crying none of this turmoil would be happening. Destiny heard her mother going off on Emma. She then heard her mother say, your mother-in-law convinced you to do it!!! Courtney said, "That evil witch, if she wasn't dead, I would kill her!! Yes, Emma admitted it was never her idea, but she was at her wits end at what to do to stop Destiny from crying. The conversation Courtney had with Emma was definitely an eye opener. Courtney decided to forgive her. When her Mom emerged from the room, Destiny pounced on her Mother. Destiny asked her Mom if she was okay. Courtney decided to share the conversation she had with her aunt. Courtney told Destiny never be afraid to tell her if something traumatic ever happens to her again.

Destiny really felt safe now. She knew that she could tell her mother things that weren't so comfortable that happened to her. Destiny felt a huge amount of relief. She had been keeping something from her mother that now was out in the open.

When Destiny turned five, she noticed that she had dreams that came true. She saw and knew things before they happened. She would later see the tragedy 911 unfold in front of her about 10 years before it actually happened. She didn't know what was going on, so she talked to her Mom. Thank God, her Mom could tell her that she had a prophetic gift. Destiny's Mom would read her Bible stories every night since she was old enough to listen and comprehend. When her Mom told her, it was a gift from God it helped a little. She was still confused. She wandered why God would give her such a gift. She didn't feel worthy. Her Mom told her that gifts come without repentance. Destiny asked her Mom, "What does that mean?" It means God has given everyone gifts and talents. We don't have to be perfect. We were born with our gifts.

As the years went on Destiny loved and sometimes disliked her gifts, because she would dream of people having babies. Destiny felt it was a blessing to be able to see that God was giving people a miracle and that she was part of their awesome experience. What a blessing to be able to see that God was giving them a miracle. The dreams about people dying would always be the hard part of accepting her gift.

Her mother made sure she knew she had black girl magic before the term was coined years later. Destiny was proud of her heritage. Her Aunt Diana and parents both marched with Dr. Martin Luther King during the Civil Right Movement. She realized that her Mom sought out Black people who were prosperous, so she could show her children that Black people held professional positions. Her mother wanted Destiny to see that black people can have many different occupations. Her Mom had a black dentist, Destiny and her brother had a black pediatrician and the family grew up with two phenomenal black businessmen.

She loved her black community and her parents built up her self-confidence every chance they got. Her mother was friends with the founder of Ebony, Mr. John H. Johnson.

Destiny's Dad's side of the family had a family reunion and they toured his facility.

Destiny loved the Hair Industry and knew she would find a place in that world. She wasn't talented enough to do hair, but she would gather hair magazines and read books and learn everything she could about hair. She definitely had a love hate relationship with her hair. She was so upset that her soft curly hair would fall when she tried to wear her Afro. Her mother started putting her hair into 2 Afro puffs. She thought it was cute at first until that seemed to be the only style her Mom knew. Then when Afros started to play out here comes the dreaded straightening comb. Destiny would hate the heat coming from the comb. Her hair was thin and soft, that is why the heat seemed like it burned her scalp. She couldn't wait to get a relaxer.

Destiny had bigger problems then getting her hair relaxed. She overheard her parents talking about a new addition to the family. Destiny wondered what effect this would have on her family. Destiny knew the secret was related to her Mom's baby sister. Then the unthinkable happened, her Mom's sister had a baby. When Destiny's Mom told her and Ed Jr. that she had a surprise for them they were elated. Destiny's Aunt Elaine always spoiled them rotten. They knew that they would be getting some great toy or something special. Courtney, Edmond Sr., Destiny and Edmond Jr. got in the car and off they went to see their surprise. When they stepped into their Grandmother's house they were led into a bedroom. Her Mom said, "Look you have a new cousin." Who in the world wanted a new cousin? Destiny and Ed Jr. were like most children obsessed with their needs and wants. Ed Jr. was not pleased with his new cousin. He walked over to her baby and said," This baby can't do anything." He felt like a least if he was getting a new cousin. He could be someone we all could play with. Destiny walked over to the bassinet and said," Auntie you got the wrong baby. This baby is white!" Destiny's parents and aunt burst out laughing. They said, "He's just a little light, this is her child. Their Aunt Elaine was no longer childless. Well, Destiny thought to herself, "I still have another Aunt I can count on to continue to spoil me rotten.

After Aunt Elaine had her baby, Courtney wanted a baby. She told her husband that she wanted another Child. Edwin said, " We already have two children." "What's wrong with them"? Courtney replied, nothing but they are getting older." "I want a baby." Edwin was not pleased with the idea. He came from a family of 9 kids. He liked their small family. He did usually give into his wife and this was no exception.

Ed Jr. and Destiny were always eavesdropping on personal conversations that their parents had. They heard their parents saying that Courtney was going to have a baby. Then Destiny thought I can now have someone to boss around like my big brother did to me. When her Mom made the announcement that she was pregnant with a baby, Destiny acted surprised and happy. There were a lot of mixed emotions after all she was the baby. Now she would be the dreaded middle child. She wasn't special anymore. She wouldn't be the baby anymore and what if Mom had a girl? Destiny would no longer be the only girl. Destiny decided she would be the smart one. No one would take that from her. This is where her thoughts of "I have to be perfect" first started. This thought of perfection would rule and even ruin some aspects of her life. Did she even realize where her wanting to be perfect came from? The answer to that question was no at first. She would realize it later in life that perfection can never be attained, unless you are Jesus Christ and she certainly was not.

Destiny was never worried about being jealous of her Baby Sister or Brother, but she did feel like the attention she was getting from her Mother would be divided into 3 kids now. She knew that her Aunt on her Mom's side of the family and her youngest Aunt on her Dad's side of the family would always give her special attention. Destiny and Ed Jr. fell in love with their new little cousin Brian. Destiny learned a valuable lesson on how she can still receive love from someone even if she has to share it with someone else. Ed Jr. was very protective over his cousin. Destiny was five years older than Brian she and Edmond Jr. always protected him every chance they got.

Destiny was very observant and analytical, not in a mathematical sense but she would break different things down and examined different scenarios. She would try to figure things out before she asked her parents. She hated it when she couldn't figure things out. Her brother Ed Jr.'s personality was totally different. Whenever something popped in his head, he asked questions right away. Ed Jr. was very inquisitive. Whereas, Destiny was curious she did her own research and Ed Jr. would go ask Courtney.

She saw how hardworking both her parents were. Destiny's Dad was a Man's Man. She would hear her Mom say that. She wondered what that meant. Then she finally figured it out. Her Dad would mentor men who were down on their luck. He would give them jobs. Several of the men he mentored went on to work full-time at other jobs. He was the reason some black men could get benefits from their jobs and take care of their families. He taught them skills that garnered them high paying wages. She figured this is what her Mom was talking about. Many of his friends and family admired him. Her Dad had been working since he was eight years old.

His mother didn't know he was shining shoes when he was eight years old. She thought he was outside playing, not on the north side of Chicago shining shoes. Ed Sr. always knew that he had to be back on the Westside before the streetlights came on so his mother wouldn't become suspicions of him working. Destiny admired his work ethic when she would hear him tell his "work stories". Destiny definitely had a love/hate relationship with her Dad. He was always so strict. He was also super overprotective of her and her siblings. She didn't realize that he cared about her and he was being a good father.

People used different coping mechanisms to manage their lives and drinking was one way her Dad managed his issues. She noticed that her Dad would drink a lot when he got stressed out. She hated when he would be verbally abusive and sometimes violent to her Mom. She hated when he would get drunk. He would curse her or anybody in his way out. She decided when he was drunk, she would stay out of his way. Destiny never wanted to be married to a man that was an alcoholic. Destiny realized that sometimes no matter how you try to escape certain people you may still end up with them. Destiny would learn later in life that people used different coping to manage their lives and drinking was one way her Dad managed his issues.

That's why Destiny was confused that even though her Dad drank. He never let his addiction interfere with bills being paid in the Scott home. Yes, Mr. and Mrs. Scott made sure every bill was paid on time. He was a great Husband and Dad when it came to taking care of his family. It's a shame when it came to taking care of is health he wasn't as diligent. Courtney made sure that she cooked for her husband. It was better for his health for him to be put on a strict diet because he would sneak and eat foods he was not suppose to eat.

Destiny heard her parents arguing. She hated for them to argue because it would become very heated. Her Mom refused to back down and her Dad did too. She would often hear her Dad say to leave him alone, but Mom needed her point heard. Destiny thought when she got married. She would leave her husband alone when he asked her to. Courtney wanted him to stop managing a famous singer. Her

Dad was very good at managing people after all he ran his own construction business and was a teacher.

The managing became a problem because this led to late hours and hanging out with people her Mom thought were seedy. Her Mom would go with him to the night clubs sometimes, but she hated it. She had to be up in the morning to attend church. She was the Minister of Music at her Baptist Church and felt she should not be hanging out all night. The last straw was when she became pregnant for the third time. She realized she would no longer be able to hang out with Edmond Sr. like before. Edmond Sr. was a very nice-looking man. She didn't trust the ladies in the clubs around her husband. She was not an insecure woman, but she wasn't crazy either. Her Mother always told her never hand your husband over to another woman.

Edmond convinced Courtney to let him keep managing. She agreed for a little while, because the singer he was managing named Gary had a record that was being played on the radio. The radio play garnered Gary a lot of attention. Edmond was constantly setting up performances at various venues in the Chicago area. Courtney felt bad she didn't want to ruin Edmond's success. Edmond would always make sure Courtney was feeling okay during her pregnancy so he could keep working with his artist.

Edmond Sr. tried to even help with the children, which he rarely did. One day Destiny and Edmond came home from school on a Friday. Edmond Sr. decided to be the model citizen by spending time with his children. He took Destiny and her brother with him to set up some singing engagements for his Singer Gary. The problem was he neglected to tell Courtney where the children were and where he was. He should have left her a note, but Edmond was to cool to leave a note. The first stop was a night club. The children were able to go in the night club because they weren't open to the public yet. They then went to Soul Train. The Soul Train Dance show started in Chicago in 1970 and aired on WCIU-TV before the show moved to California. Destiny was in awe of her Dad talking to Don Cornelius about his singer being on the show. After all she watched Mr. Cornelius on television every week. When they first arrived at the show they were taping. Destiny remember trying to see the dancers dancing through the peep hole at the door. Unfortunately, the door was too high for her to see without her jumping up and down to view anything. She started jumping up and down and then she was able to see the teenagers dancing. She was beyond excited. When they finally arrived home, Courtney was not happy. It was after 10pm and she wanted to know where her children were. Edmond knew this would not be good for him. When he told Courtney where he was. She screamed, "You had my kids in a Nightclub"? He tried to explain what he was doing but she was furious. When she finally calmed down, he told her the Club wasn't even open. Edmond also explained that Courtney was always complaining that he never spent quality time with his kids. He decided since it was Friday and they didn't have school the next day this would be the perfect time to hang out with his children. Destiny's Dad always knew how to calm her Mom down. Courtney told him it's me or this showbiz thing you have going on. He chose his family.

It was Easter and Destiny couldn't wait to wear her new clothes and yes get her hair done. Her Mom told her children that the next day after school they may have another sister or brother coming home. Her Mom was right her sister Carrie was born. Her brother, Edmond Jr., was ticked off. Destiny's Mom always knew how to make her children happy. She told Ed Jr. that Carrie looked like him. She had the same coloring the Edmond Jr. had. He instantly changed his feelings on his new little baby Sister. Destiny was actually happy. She had a little sister and she now had someone to boss around. Destiny also decided it was now time to come out of her shell. She was shy and quiet at first. She noticed her friends would try to run her over. She was a big sister now. She might have to defend her baby sister at some point. The new Destiny was more powerful, spoke her mind and demanded to be respected.

Destiny's Dad never really took care of his children by himself. When his wife was in the hospital for a hysterectomy, he hired Darlene one of the Scott's adult young neighbors to cook, clean and take care of his children's every need. Destiny was glad that her Dad hired her favorite babysitter, Darlene. She was so pretty and nice. All Edmond Jr. did was stare at her. Destiny knew Ed Jr. had a crush on her even though she was 20 years old and Ed Jr. was only 9 years old. Destiny was always thinking on her feet. She knew that if she did this favor for Ed Jr. by asking her Dad to hire Darlene. Ed Jr. would be in her debt for a little while. Ed Jr. was always doing something mean to his little sister like pushing her down a flight of stairs for no good reason. She wanted to earn some brownie points from her brother.

Destiny first thought of her baby sister as a little intruder. She came to love her just as she had done 3 years earlier when her cousin Brian was born. Destiny always knew she was her Dad's favorite. Destiny looked so much like Edmond's beautiful Mother Maria. Edmond's Mom had this beautiful soft hair that felt like cotton when you touched it. Maria's grandfather was Caucasian. When Carrie came along Destiny's Father all but ignored her. She wasn't jealous but she felt like she was being replaced by Carrie. Destiny was always understanding but she did have a bit of a temper. She would never hurt her baby sister, but her Dad was letting this little kid get away with murder. Little Carrie grew into a sassy little child. She would tell you to kiss her butt in a minute. She was a hot mess. Edmond Sr. thought everything she did was cute.

Her grandmother warned her Dad that it was wrong to show some much favoritism to his baby girl Carrie. Maria told Edmond that if he didn't reprimand Carrie, Destiny and Edmond Jr. would end up disliking her. Courtney tried to get through to Edmond. Edmond ignored everything Courtney said about the way he allowed Carrie to get away with her bad behavior. Courtney finally had to involve Edmond's Mom. Edmond Sr. really looked up to his mother and paid attention to everything his mother told him about how to live his life. The reason Courtney was desperate to help her children was because Carrie had turned into a spoiled brat. Carrie had started lying on her siblings and cousins. She would say they hit her when she was sleep, stole her money and punched her every chance they got. These accusations weren't true, but Edmond Sr. believed every word out of Carrie's mouth. Courtney knew she had to take action. Carrie's lying had really gotten out of hand. Edmond did listen to his mother and finally the lying subsided in the Scott household.

What made matters even worse than Carrie lying was the fact that Carrie had an awesome gift. Carries was a dynamic singer. Destiny came from a musical family. Everyone on her mother's side of the family could sing. The family discovered that Carrie had a fantastic voice when she was about 4 years old. The family knew her voice was special, and her Mom even compared her to her sister Diana. Destiny really felt out of place, because she felt that she didn't possess any talent. She could hold a note but nothing like her powerhouse baby sister. Her brother was an awesome artist and could fix anything. Destiny started to wonder what she could do. That's when she realized she was smart. A light bulb went off in her head she would be the well-behaved perfect kid with the good grades. She didn't realize that perfection would never come to her. In fact, it would drive people away from her instead of making them love her!

When she was in the third grade, she had a teacher named Mrs. Smith. Destiny loved Mrs. Smith; she would tell her that she was a smart child. She would often tell the other kids to develop study habits like Destiny. Destiny asked Mrs. Smith to stop using her in examples, because she didn't want to be deemed as the teacher's pet. When it was time for Destiny to go to the fourth grade Mrs. Smith placed Destiny in the gifted class. Destiny was livid, because now she was no longer the smartest kid in the class. Those children were super intelligent. She stayed with them until she graduated from eighth grade. Destiny was able to also attend Freshmen English class at Percy L. Julian while she was still in eighth grade. The name of the program was called Early Involvement.

It did help that Courtney never had favorites. Courtney had a way of making all of her children feel like they were number one. All the children thought they were her favorite. She would say, "Mom loves you all the same and I don't have any favorites." She would say that her children were her life. Courtney's children actually believed her. She could make anything she was doing with her children and for her children exciting to them. She was very good at hyping them up. She was their own personal hype lady. Her children loved her so much.

CHAPTER 2

The Discovery Years

---•◦•---

Destiny definitely needed to find her place in the family, because she was now the dreaded middle child. Yes, she did have the middle child syndrome for a little while. Destiny caught a break. Carrie and Edmond Jr. were a lot alike. They were so much more mischievous than Destiny. Carrie was Sassy and Edmond Jr. was always getting phone calls, bad notes regarding his disruptive behavior from his teachers. His grades in school were horrible. The grading school in elementary school was: E = Excellent, G= Good, F= Fair and U= Unsatisfactory. Edmond received mostly F's and U's; he only got a G for his gym grade. Destiny knew that if she never got bad reports from school and received good grades. She would surely look good in her parent's eyes. She yearned for their approval which she received. She even decided to speak to her Mom about standardized testing. She knew her Mom was a High School Music Teacher and she had a high IQ. She figured her Mom could tutor her on how to score well on the standardized test in school. Destiny was able to do well on standardized test because of the help her Mother gave her.

Courtney was the Minister of Music at their Baptist Church. The Church was a staple in their lives. The church the family attended is where Courtney and Edmond met as children and fell in love as young adults. She believed if you start off a child early with morals they would not depart from those teachings. Courtney instilled morals and standards in her children. Destiny was taught Christian values and loved God and wanted to be baptized. She spoke with her brother and they both decided it was time to surrender their lives to Christ. Destiny was 5 years old and Edmond was 6 years old. Destiny didn't really understand everything about accepting Jesus Christ as her personal Savior. She attended an excellent church with an excellent Sunday School. The Sunday school she attended taught her a lot and as time went on. She learned what surrendering your life to Christ meant. Destiny's

Christian walk was basically molded by her Mom and the church she attended.

Her paternal grandfather was a Pastor. They didn't attend his church, but the family attended church every week like clockwork. Her Father would often sneak over to his cousin's house because they lived next door to the church. Destiny's Father's Cousin Maria who was the namesake of Destiny's Grandmother and her Sister Edna were fantastic cooks. Destiny was blessed because her Mom was a great cook and a lot of people in her family cooked well. If Courtney didn't see her husband after church, she knew where he was. She would tell Destiny," Go next door and get your Father." Destiny would step in the house and smell the delicious aroma of food cooking. She would announce to her Dad it was time to go home. His female cousins attended church, but their husband didn't and Edmond was good friends with them as well.

Destiny actually appreciated the fact that they were being raised in church except for one thing, too many afternoon programs. In the Baptist church in the 60's, 70's, 80's and 90's there were too many afternoon programs. Destiny already attended Sunday school, then church service and she usually had to attend another service later that day. Wow Destiny felt it was team too much. She loved God but she felt this was way too much for her attending all of these services. Courtney met some very good friends at church. She joined the children's choir. She had choir rehearsal on Saturday afternoon and she discovered it was another opportunity to spend time with her friends.

Her parents had their share of issues, but they were a great example of how two people with the help of God survived marriage in this society. Destiny was blessed with great examples of marriage. All of her Aunts and Uncles were married at some point in their lives. Some of the marriage weren't successful but at least Destiny saw examples of what to do and what not to do when it came to relationships. Destiny's Mom always admonished her daughter never to act like a wife if you were a girlfriend. Destiny asked her Mom what that meant. She said never to live with a man without marriage, and don't have sex or children out of wedlock. She said some women want to get married, but if a person wants that for themselves. They shouldn't act like they are already married. She always remembered that and she felt that was why she was treated a certain way by men. She never allowed a man to mistreat her.

Her parents started an organization called the Spring Trip Committee. This organization was started so African American high school students could travel all over the world during their Spring Break from school. Destiny and her brother Edmond were able to travel all over the world with their parents. The main students that went on the trips attended Calumet High School. The Scotts gave the best parties, traveled all over the world and attended different events around the city. Destiny started to notice that her friends on the block were being mean to her. She decided to talk to her Mother about the situation. Her Mother told her that usually, if you haven't done anything to provoke your friends and family they may be jealous. This broke Destiny's heart. She loved going outside to play. She really didn't know how to handle this situation. She decided that she would just stop going outside. Her brother experienced some of the same treatment, but he ignored it and found friends that accepted him for who he was. Destiny was very close to her brother. She asked him why he still went outside. When Edmond Jr. or as she affectionately called him Ed told her how he handled haters. She said, "I will do the same thing." Which is to find friends who care for her and were not jealous. She was back going outside before the summer ended. Luckily, Destiny had many friends in the surrounding area. As long as she was home before dark, she was free to visit them all. Her brother did give good advice sometimes.

Destiny decided it was time to revisit the whole relaxer subject again. She convinced her Mom to give her a relaxer because they were going to California to visit her uncle. She told her Mom "It's hot there and my hair is going to sweat into a soft Afro puff". She had just turned 14 years old and it made her feel really grown up. Her persistence paid off, it worked she allowed Destiny to get the relaxer.

Destiny's brother was always getting into trouble at school. He was a year older than Destiny. They attended the same high school. Courtney asked Edmond Sr. to go up to the school to speak with his teachers because she was tired of Ed's awful behavior. Edmond Sr. came up with a plan to curb his son's terrible behavior. Destiny saw her Dad wake her brother up one morning and take him on a car ride. When they came home Edmond's behavior began to drastically change for the good. He graduated a year early. It took ten years for Destiny to find out where her Dad took her brother. He took him to skid row. Skid row was where the homeless people lived. He told his son that if he kept acting crazy that is where he would end up. Edmond Sr. knew he couldn't keep whipping Edmond Jr. All his life so he came up with some different punishment. One-time Edmond Jr. was torturing Destiny with snake. She told her Dad and he made him do a 10-page paper on snakes. He wanted Edmond Jr. to learn several valuable lessons; the snake could have been poisonous, he could have been killed, and Destiny could have been killed.

Destiny's parents were very protective, but she was so happy that they started letting her take the bus after all she was a freshman in High school. She would go to the show at Evergreen Plaza or shop there. She wasn't allowed to date yet, but she could hang out with her female friends as long as her parents knew where she was. Destiny's Mother didn't play when it came to her checking in. There were no cell phones in 1977. Destiny had to check in by calling her Mother if their plans changed or if she would get home later than the time. She had to use a pay phone if she was not at one of her friend's house. She was embarrassed that she had to check in but if she didn't there would be hell to pay when she arrived home. She didn't want to be put on punishment, so she went along with the rules.

Destiny wanted to go to the homecoming Dance with a date. Her over the top strict Father was not having it. She thought I'm now 15 years old and a sophomore at Percy L. Julian. She decided she would go with her best friend and they would just hook up with their dates at the dance. She felt like Cinderella because her Mom dropped her off at her best friend Dena's house. Destiny had to be back by 12 midnight. The dance was over at 11:00pm and she told her Mom they would grab a snack after the dance. She would meet her Mom back at Dena's house. Destiny begged her Mom to let Dena drop her off at home. Courtney said, "Maybe your Junior or Senior year but no, not yet!"

Dena had the coolest Dad. He purchased an older car for her. It was a 1972 Chevrolet Impala. She wasn't even 16 years old. She was 15 years old like me. In order to obtain your license a person had to be 16 years old. She still had her learners permit. When a person has their permit, they are supposed to drive with a licensed driver. We made it to the party and we had a ball!! Dena's younger sister Rena was the same age as my younger sister and they were best friends. My Mom had dropped Destiny's Sister off at Dena's house as well. Carrie loved going out when I was out it made her feel like she was a teenager especially staying out late at night.

Courtney was very proud of Destiny. Destiny excelled in high school. She was on the honor roll her Junior and Senior year, a member of Dancers Incorporated Dance Team, Future Business Leaders of America (FBLA) and Office Occupations. She also had a job downtown at the Sears Tower that she started after her junior year and she worked there until the end of her senior year. Courtney kept her word, she told

Destiny if she kept up her grades she could work and do other activities. She and Edmond did relax some of their rules. Courtney really had a way with her husband. She was great at convincing Edmund to follow her lead. She made him believe he was in control when really, she was taking the lead on something's. She made him think it was his idea.

Destiny noticed her brother was sneaking off somewhere without telling anyone where he was going. He finally let Destiny in on his secret. He told her he was leaving the house for good a day before his 18th birthday. Destiny asked him if Mom and Dad knew he was leaving and he told her no. Destiny told him if he didn't tell their Mom she would. When he told Courtney, she was devastated. She cried for months after her son left. Edmond returned after basic training for a short visit. He stayed in the Marines for 3 years. He landed in Southern California after leaving the Marines and never lived in Chicago again. He decided to complete his college education at Chapman College in Orange, California. He earned a Bachelor's in Biological Sciences. He would go on to earn a master's degree in Engineering.

Edmond Jr. had a love/hate relationship with his Father. He knew he could never live in the same town with him. He never agreed with his excessive drinking. Edmond Jr. would often tell his Father he needed to stop because he was ruining his health. He looked up to him, but their relationship was very volatile. He had a fight with him a couple of months before he enrolled in the Marines. He felt leaving home for good was the solution to his problems. Their relationship did improve after Edmond Jr. moved away.

Destiny was so excited because it was finally her senior year and yes prom time. Her favorite colors were pink and blue. She decided to wear a powder blue prom dress. There was a seamstress at her church that made the most beautiful clothes she had ever seen. Destiny purchased her pattern and material for her dress. Since, she was now employed Destiny paid for everything. She also designed her jacket she would be wearing with the dress. Since Destiny couldn't date until she was 18 years old. She was wandering who would be her prom date. She decided to ask one of the young men at Calumet High School. Calumet High School was where her Mother taught. Courtney was a Music Teacher and had a Gospel Chorus. Courtney allowed Destiny to sing with her choir whenever they performed outside of the school. They would travel to different churches in the Chicago area and perform at different church programs. Destiny didn't realize one of her Mom's students was watching her. He zeroed in on Destiny almost as soon as he saw her come to school with her Mom. In September after one of their performances David found his way over to Destiny. The whole choir went to a restaurant to eat. David sat down and started to talk to Destiny. He was about 6'4, had medium brown skin color, beautiful white teeth and he was a very intelligent young man. Destiny was mesmerized by how cool he was. David definitely had this cool swag working for him. He told her he worked at a liquor store. Destiny was wandering to herself wasn't he too young to work at a liquor store? After all David was only 17 years old like me, which meant he wasn't even old enough to drink alcohol let alone sell it. His boss turned a blind eye to the age issue and let him work there. He always had a lot of money and he didn't mind spending it on Destiny. He asked Destiny for her phone number and she gave it to him. Destiny asked him right there at the table if he could escort her to prom. David smiled and said," I would love to escort you to prom." Destiny almost melted, then reality set in, how was she going to tell her Mom that she was going to prom with one of her students. She was scared to tell my Mom because he was her student and he had her home number now.

She finally told her Mom and of course she almost went into cardiac arrest. Courtney said, "You did what?" "You gave him our home number?" Destiny told Courtney her concerns and she decided to ask David. She told her Mom she needed a prom date and since Dad and Edmond Jr. had practically scared every guy that liked her away. She didn't have a lot of options. As Destiny stood in front of her Mother looking terrified her Mother did something she didn't expect. She started laughing. She said "You poor baby, yes it's okay to talk to David. You have had a rough time with your Father and Brother when it comes to dating, especially boys at your school. Destiny could always talk to her Mom. She was blunt but she was at least easy to reason with whereas; her Father was not reasonable most of the time.

Now, they just had to break the news to Edmond Sr. Courtney told Destiny she would tell him that David had to call Destiny in order to get everything together for prom. Her Father actually took the news better than they thought. Edmond said," I will allow her to talk to him, but only about prom"!! Destiny was like is this man serious. We can only talk about prom, that would be hard if not almost impossible. She prayed her Dad wouldn't be at home when David called. After all her Dad was a workaholic and was not home a lot. Her prayers were answered. Her Dad was only home one time when David called. David was attentive to her at first like most guys are when they first start a relationship with a lady. They discussed what color they were wearing, what time the prom started and how much they missed each other. She couldn't wait for the prom to come. She paid for her hair, nails, dress, shoes and prom tickets. David asked if she needed help, but she said no. He had his own prom and she didn't want to burden him with her bills. Courtney was also willing to help her pay for prom, but Destiny was always a proud person and didn't ask for any help. Destiny told David he could pay for their activities after the prom. They had planned to go to dinner and a party after prom.

Prom day was finally here. She always remembered the date May 22, 1981. May 22nd was her brother's birthday. He was away serving in the Marines. She hated that he wouldn't be able to see her off to prom. Edmond Jr. didn't go to his prom, so her parents were excited as well since it was their first child attending prom. David was getting a black tuxedo made. He called earlier and told Destiny he was on his way to pick up his tuxedo. Destiny said, "Okay, I will see you at 6:00pm sharp". He said," No problem see you then".

Well, 6:00pm came and went no David. Destiny didn't receive a phone call and an hour passed she started to worry. Finally, he arrived at 7:30pm. She was livid. When she found out he wasn't in a horrible accident, she went totally off on him. He just looked at her and said the guy wasn't finished making his tuxedo, so he had to go rent another one and the only tuxedo they had was a baby blue tuxedo. It was the exact same shade as her gown. They were late but they looked adorable. Her anger subsided once she heard the story. Her parents decided they wanted to do a photo shoot, but she was ready to be on her way to the prom. They took a few snapshots and they left. Once in the car, David told her he needed to pick up his friend Steven and drop him off at his prom. Steven attended Lindbloom High School and his prom was in Downtown Chicago so it shouldn't be a big deal. Destiny thought to herself, "No it wouldn't have been a big deal to drop his fried off if he was on time. "Destiny's prom was at the Hilton Hotel Downtown. Destiny couldn't believe he had the nerve to make 2 stops before they made it to her prom. What David did was a total turn off and selfish to her, this was her prom. She didn't blame him for his suit not being ready, but to be almost 2 hours late and then want to make stops wasn't fair to her. David had also stopped calling her as much all he did was work. She wanted to go to the show or out to eat but he was never available. He never seems to have time for her anymore. She decided that their relationship was over after the prom. Destiny didn't put up with a lot of shenanigans from anyone.

When they finally arrived, she looked for her best friend Dena. Dena was such a sweetheart she saved them a seat and made sure they had all of their food. Dena liked David because he was suave and cool. Dena had arrived in a limousine with her date, but she wanted to leave with us. Destiny was cool with letting them hang with them for the evening. They went to Lawry's Restaurant in downtown Chicago. After dining there they went to a party and had the time of our lives. Destiny didn't arrive home until 5: 30 a.m.

Destiny was aware that some girls lost their virginity on prom night. Destiny considered herself to be a good Christian young lady and was still a virgin. She was proud of the fact she remained a virgin while in High School. She was also worried about getting pregnant. David was a total gentleman; he didn't even try to deflower Destiny. He only kissed her when he dropped her off and it was their first kiss after being together for 8 months. She was over him after the whole being late for prom incident. Years later after dealing with the horrible men she dealt with, she felt she may have been too hard on David.

Destiny turned 18 years old June 5th and graduated June 14, 1981. She was excited, single and ready to mingle. Destiny had a conversation with her Father, and he told her he would no longer be a thorn in her side. He told her, "You are now 18 years old. I have raised you the best way I know how. You can do what you want to do within reason. Well after being restrained for so long Destiny lost her mind. She said to herself, "Finally freedom from my parents what is a girl to do!!" She started dating about 10 guys at one time. She wasn't a whore. She barely kissed these guys. She no longer had to sneak and go on dates. She was free to have guys calling her house without hoping her Father wasn't home. Her Father still did little things like mix up the guy's name if guys called and she wasn't at home. He almost got her in trouble. She had a friend named John that liked her. John called but her Dad told her Deno called. Thank God that Deno was just a friend. She still was a virgin but dating and being able to receive phone calls at home was like a dream come true for Destiny.

One beautiful hot summer day in June the doorbell rang. When Destiny opened the door she saw the finest specimen standing there in front of her asking could he cut their grass. His name was Philander. She called him Phil for short. Since Destiny's brother left home Destiny and her Mother had tried to cut the grass. They both hated it. This was an answer to a prayer. Courtney told him she would have to ask her husband. Phil begged her but she told him to come back tomorrow. Edmond said no at first, but Courtney sweet talked him into letting Phil cut the grass.

When Phil returned Courtney told him he had the job. Phil asked Destiny out the same day he returned to cut the grass. She played him at first, but he kept asking so she finally relented. She found out he was a year older than her and had been in the same class as her brother when they attended William H. Ryder, the neighborhood school. Destiny did feel like it was love at first sight. She didn't have a whole lot of dating experience. Her first kiss took place at church after choir rehearsal. She was 15 years old and the guy was 17 years old. She thought Chuck was nice looking and talented. He was a musician and he played for the Youth Choir. He broke up with her because her Dad wouldn't let them go out. He never really said it was over, he just started ignoring her and when she asked him why he told her that her Dad was the reason. She had a couple of guys in the neighborhood that tried to talk to her, but it was either her cousin, brother or father that ruined it.

Phil was way more experienced than Destiny. When she told him that she was a virgin he didn't even believe her. She told him that she was very old fashioned that she had to be in love with the guy and she needed to make sure the guy wasn't just using her for sex. She told him he would have to wait 6 months to be with her sexually. Usually after dealing with her family and not getting the goodies her boyfriends lasted about a month if they lasted that long it was a miracle. Destiny realized most girls her age was sexually active the guys she dated were usually good looking and popular. She gave up on trying to compete in the sex arena, so she developed this unstoppable personality. She knew someone would fall in love with her one day.

Destiny noticed that not only was Phil still around. He never pressured her for sex. She thought they would be together forever, so she finally slept with him. He then introduced her to oral sex and now there was no letting go of her soon to be husband. She had nothing to compare her sex life too, but she was blissfully happy being with Phil. He always respected her and treated her well. Destiny would soon discover he wasn't as wonderful as she thought he was!!

CHAPTER 3

College Life

----··•·•··----

Since both of her parents were educators Destiny knew she had to attend college, but she was scared out of her mind to attend college. She was accepted at every college she applied to. She was going to attend Northern University in Dekalb, IL. but she lost her nerve, so she chooses to attend Olive Harvey in Chicago, IL.

She was walking down the street in her Southside neighborhood and she heard these two girls talking about her fiancée. They were saying he got another girl pregnant. Destiny didn't know what to believe. She knew they knew who she was. She just kept walking like she never heard them. When she arrived at school she couldn't concentrate. She told her best friend Dena. Dena told her, "When you get home call him and ask him". Dena was always there for her when she needed her. She was her voice of reason. Dena was blunt like

Destiny's Mom and Destiny's Cousin Dee. Destiny always thought that was a good personality trait. They were all strong women. Destiny gathered her strength from these three women in her life.

Destiny had just finished her freshmen year in college. She was on the honor roll and everything was going well, until she was forced to confront the gossip in the Gresham neighborhood in Chicago. She dialed Phil's number and when he answered they just had a general conversation then she asked him the burning question. Do you have a baby on the way? He already told me he had 1 child already. I accepted it because it was before we met. An older woman had seduced him while he was cutting her Mom's grass. She was 24 years old and he was 16 years old. He answered me and said yes. I was stunned. He acted like it was no big deal. Destiny screamed "We are talking about getting married and you got some Chick pregnant?" "Who does that Destiny exclaimed!! Phil had the nerve to tell her that she wasn't putting out, so he had sex with this random girl in the neighborhood. Destiny was furious but you said you would wait for me Destiny exclaimed!! You're a liar and a cheat Destiny felt her Father's personality taking her over, he loved to use curse words to express himself. It was something Destiny only did when she was upset. She cursed Phil out for about 5 minutes and hung up on him. He tried calling her back, but she just kept hanging up on him. This was her first really big heartbreak.

Phil later told Destiny he cried when he knew he lost her. Destiny ran into Phil years later and he told Destiny how horrible his life had been since he became involved with the girl, he cheated on her with. His ex-wife was a total lunatic. She told him "I'm not saying what you did was right but damn, next time use protection Dude! He later told Destiny the girl's Father made them get married. The Father threatened to have Phil arrested for raping his daughter. Phil was devastated he would never rape anyone but because he was 19 years old and his daughter was only 16 years old the Father knew it would not be that hard to press rape charges on Phil. It was a shot gun wedding. He was married to her for 20 years and he said they were only together for about 3 years. She cheated on him numerous of times with friends and other men. She was strung out on drugs most of the time they were together.

When Destiny first heard not only did Phil cheat on her, but he impregnated another teenage girl she was furious. She was not only furious, but first she wanted revenge. Destiny use to have a T-Shirt that read, "I Don't Get Mad I Get Even. She had grown spiritually and realized she would let God fight her battles. Destiny would tell people her favorite quote from the Bible Hebrews 10:30 "For we know him who said, "Vengeance is Mine, I will repay," says the Lord. And again, The Lord will judge his people." Destiny wanted to pay him back for hurting her but she just let it go. She knew God would handle Phil. Destiny decided to move on with her life, she was young and not going to let what Phil did stop her from finding true love.

While attending Olive Harvey her sophomore year, she met this guy name Herb. He was gorgeous, 6'4, thin and light and very intelligent. He was soft spoken but still knew how to command attention. Destiny never really liked light skin guys, but they sure liked her. Herb was a great guy. He was such a gentleman. Edmond Sr. even liked him, of course he still gave Herb a hard time. One-time, Destiny and Herb were sitting on the porch talking and her Dad was coming home from work. Destiny said, "Hi Dad" and of course he spoke, but when Herb said, Hi Mr. Scott", he ignored him. Destiny was so embarrassed, but she told Herb that's just the way her Dad was. Destiny was ticked off at her Dad and after Herb left, she confronted her Dad and asked him why he was so rude? He claimed he never heard Herb speak to him. Destiny knew he was not being honest, but she couldn't do anything with her crazy Father.

Herb didn't have a lot of money, but he still tried to take Destiny out for lunch whenever he could afford it. Destiny told him he didn't always have to pay for her, but he wasn't having that, he said a real man pays his and his woman's way. As the year was closing, Herb announced he was going to Howard University in Washington, DC. Destiny was devastated even though they weren't in love and never had a sexual relationship. They had deep feelings for each other. He still kept in touch with Destiny, but they decided to date other people. Destiny decided to transfer to Chicago State in Chicago, IL .

Edmond was very close to his family. They always lived within close proximity of each other. Edmond's Brother decided he wanted to move to the Country Club Hills, which is in the South Suburbs of Illinois. His brother Rob was building a house in Country Club Hills, IL. Rob wanted Edmond to move but of course Edmond had to clear it with Courtney. Courtney was game because even though the house she lived in currently was a new house when she moved in it. She never had a formal dining room and that's what she wanted. The new houses were expensive at that time $100,000 for a house was a lot of money. The two brothers were doing very well financially so they could afford to move into County Club Hills, IL.

The new houses were beautiful. When Destiny's Mom told her, they were moving she was so upset. After all she grew up in the City of Chicago. She didn't know anyone in the South Suburbs. She didn't have a car so she would be stuck out there. This was the worst news in the world for the 20-

year-old college student. Destiny was happy for her Parents, but sad for herself. Courtney to the rescue again, she told Destiny that since she was moving away from her friends. she could have her own phone line at the new home. Destiny was elated. She hated sharing a phone with her parents. She told her Mom that she was interested in moving in with her Cousin Margie. Destiny had discussed her plans with Margie and she said if she wanted to stay in Chicago she didn't mind her moving in with her. Margie only lived about 10 minutes from Chicago State. Destiny was elated. Margie called Destiny was some great news, she was getting married. Destiny was happy for Margie. After all Margie was 24 years old and wanted to get married by the time, she turned 25 years old. Margie was getting her wish. Margie also had some not so good news for Destiny. She was moving in with her Mother to save money for the wedding. Destiny was back to moving in with her Parents. She was happy that she would have her own phone line, but she still would miss living in Chicago.

Destiny was majoring in Business Administration and Marketing at Chicago State just like she was when she was at

Olive Harvey. She joined a Business Club at Chicago State in order to get to know some more people. She only knew about 3 people at Chicago State when she first started attending the school. Destiny was always a very gregarious person and loved having friends. She met a guy 2 years older than herself that she fell madly in love with at first sight. He was judging a contest she was in with her business class mates. She loved her Marketing Teacher Dr. Milner. Dr. Milner had them write a commercial. Her class then went to the Radio and Television Department to tape the commercial. Destiny's classmates chose her script. The team she was on garnered the grade of **A** for this assignment. Dr. Milner submitted their work for this contest. Destiny's group won the contest. They received a plaque. Destiny was a hustler and wished they could have received some money.

Matthew wasn't the type of guy Destiny was usually attracted to. Matthew was nice looking but a little short at 5'10 and too thin for Destiny. She saw something interesting in him so when she saw her friend Pat talking to him. Destiny intruded into their conversation. Pat picked up on the clues

Destiny was dropping and decided to walk away. Destiny smiled her winning smile and Matthew ate up everything she said. Destiny would never ask a guy for his number so after the initial conversation they parted ways.

Destiny asked Pat all kinds of questions about the gorgeous Matthew. Pat told her he was single, but she didn't know a whole lot about him except he was a Senior, a member of the fraternity Kappa Alpha Psi and he was going to law school after he graduated. He actually should have graduated because he was 2 years older than Destiny. He knew she was a business major, so he kept showing up in the Business Building. He finally asked Destiny for her number after bumping into her a couple of times. Matthew was a nerd, he was smart, a little different than most men and that intrigued Destiny. She wanted to find out everything about him.

People always tried to figure out who Destiny was, some would say she was a nerd, then some saw her as the popular girl, she hated when people tried to pigeonhole her. She didn't think anyone ever really figured out who Destiny really was. She loved that people had a hard time figuring her out. She never really wanted people to get that close to her. She only allowed a few people to get really close to her. A few friends and a few family members really knew how multifaceted this young woman was turning into.

Her friends stared to notice Destiny was never without male company. Destiny never saw herself as all that beautiful and never cared if people saw her as beautiful. She wasn't raised that way. Her Mom was a very intelligent woman and only complimented Destiny on her being intelligent. Her Dad's Sister Viola who was beautiful all her life always told Destiny she was beautiful. Destiny just assumed because she was her Aunt, she was supposed to say that. Destiny believed it was her personality that garnered her male attention. She would go out with gorgeous women and men would talk to her because her beautiful friends were acting stuck up.

College gave Destiny the freedom she always dreamed of, but it also came with responsibilities. Her parents were no nonsense about their children living up to their responsibilities. They told Destiny that they didn't care if she worked as long as she went to School and earned good grades.

Destiny was serious about passing all of her classes. Destiny was working at the Social Security Office on Western Avenue in Chicago, IL and paid for her first semester in college but she got laid off. Her Mother picked up the slack and started paying her tuition. Destiny started working for her Grandmother Alberta's bookstore. She was able to pay for her books that she needed while attending college. Destiny always had to have some income. She hated asking anyone for money.

Destiny started getting closer to Matthew and they started discussing marriage, but Destiny just wasn't ready. She wanted to finish college. Matthew was older and was ready to settle day. Destiny's Advertising Professor Dr. Milner was the Business Club's Mentor. She asked the group to accompany her to Washington, DC. She was going to visit her son. Matthew knew her and asked could he go. There were about 10 of students from Chicago State going.

The students decided to meet at Matthew's house. Destiny's Father liked Michael. He never offered any of Destiny's friend's food, but he offered Matthew his shrimp he

64

was cooking one time when he was visiting Destiny. Destiny was elated finally someone her Father actually held a conversation with that she dated, this was epic!! The students decided to meet at Matthew's house. The students decided to drive. Dr. Milner flew to D.C. Destiny needed a ride to Matthew's house and her Mother could not take her. Courtney volunteered Edmond Sr. Destiny's Dad wanted to know some details of the trip. She told him Matthew and his best friend were from wealthy families. His best friend and Fraternity brother Isaac would drive his Father's Mercedes Benz. When Edmond heard the details, he was more comfortable with Destiny going, it didn't matter that his daughter was 20 years old. He would always be protective no matter what. Destiny started thinking what happened to her being over 18 years old and able to do what she wanted?

The car unfortunately broke down on the way to Washington, DC. Mathew and Isaac had to walk several miles to get help. The other students in the other car didn't know we were stuck and our teacher flew to D.C. We finally were able to get help. We stayed in one hotel room while the car was being serviced. We woke up the next morning and the car was fixed and we were back on the road again.

All the ladies stayed in one room and all the guys stayed in one room when we were in Washington, DC. The guys always found themselves in the ladies' room. Even though Destiny was with madly in love with Matthew she never forgot about Herb. Everybody wanted to go on a D.C. tour except for Patty and Destiny. Destiny had been on a D.C. tour about 3 years prior to this trip. Destiny didn't know Patty that well, but she seemed nice. Patty was 4 years older than Destiny. She had attended Dillard University in New Orleans, LA but came back home to Chicago. She decided to finish up her college education at Chicago State. Destiny told Patty about Herb and how she wanted to connect with him. Patty was game. They made their way to Howard University. Destiny couldn't believe how beautiful the campus was. She decided that she was transferring to Howard immediately. She went to the office and collected the information for Howard. She also located Herb. She had his room number and called him. He wasn't in but his roommate took down all her information. Destiny had a ball. They flirted, took pictures with some handsome guys and toured the campus.

When they arrived back at the hotel another classmate Myra told Destiny that Herb called. All the ladies had Destiny's back. She had told the ladies that Matthew was her boyfriend. They knew that Herb was an Ex-Boyfriend. Destiny discovered that she wasn't the only one getting phones calls from Ex Partners. Matthew dated an actress about 2 years before he started dating Destiny. She called his room. He told Destiny about her. Destiny asked how she knew he was in D.C. he replied, "My Mom gave her all the information." She had called his house and his Mom answered the phone. Destiny was livid. How dare she give her the information? Destiny asked Matthew, "Didn't your Mom know I was here." He was not happy about what his Mom did, but he told Destiny, "I guess she just wasn't thinking."

Destiny was really good at listening to her gut feelings. She felt something was off with Matthew when he found out she wasn't ready to get married. The trip was during the Schools Spring break. Matthew and Destiny were always together but Matthew was not very romantic. It was a disappointment to Destiny especially since she was considering marrying him. She thought that his skills for being romantic needed much improvement. She tried to avoid having sex with him and he thought she didn't like sex. She didn't want to hurt his feelings and tell him she just wanted to wait for marriage.

Matthew graduated and moved to New York to attend Law School. He only called her once. Destiny decided to move on especially since she was transferring to Howard University. She couldn't wait to see Herb. He missed her just as much as she missed him. They picked up right where they left off in Chicago. Destiny was trying to wait for marriage, so she was not interested having anymore pre-marital sex.

Destiny realized she made a mistake by transferring to Howard University. It was a great experience, but she missed her Mom and all her friends. Herb's body type was starting to change. He was skinny at first, but when he began pledging Omega Psi Phi Fraternity he got buffed. He never forced himself on Destiny, but he didn't have to because all the women on campus were on him. He lost his damn mind. Destiny couldn't take it anymore and after a year there she was back at Chicago State University. She didn't get any bad grades and she was still on track to graduate. She found a job in the Bursar's office at Chicago State. She loved it, she no longer had to get on the bus and train to work at her grandmother's bookstore. She hated gong to the Westside of Chicago to work. Her Dad worked as a Teacher on the Westside so he would pick her up.

Herb missed Destiny he came home for Christmas break. He called her and since she had broken up with a guy named Darryl that she met at Chicago State she met up with Herb at his house. The romance with Darryl was brief it only lasted about 10 months. They broke up because they grew apart and she was now alone. She was actually surprised to hear from Herb. He acted like he could care less when she returned home to Chicago. He would later tell her that she was the only genuine female he met especially since he pledged. They only wanted to be with him because he was in a fraternity. Herb knew Destiny before he was in the fraternity. She was not fazed by him being in a Fraternity. She decided to go over his house. He seduced her and she enjoyed every moment of it. She enjoyed his company and when they got together. They didn't have to have sex they could talked all night. She was sad when he had to go back to school. She knew that she needed to concentrate on graduating. She was already a year behind with all of the transferring she did. She finally finished in the summer of 1986.

Destiny was so happy that both sets of her Grandparents knew she was attending college. Sadly, her Fathers Dad died her junior year. He would never see her graduate. Pastor Robert Scott was born in 1898. He had attended college in Mississippi. This was very rare in those days for a Black man to attend college. He didn't graduate but she was just proud of the fact he attended college. He was so proud of Destiny as well. He was an editor for a newspaper editor. He was 86 years old when he passed way. Her Mother's parents and her Father's Mother saw her graduate from College. Sadly, her Grandmother Maria passed away at the age of 76 of breast cancer at the end of 1986. She was super close to her Grandmother. She now only had her Mother's parents left.

Destiny's obtained a job right before graduation. Her friend Pat from Chicago State had also graduated and obtained a great Marketing job. Pat offered her a position working on her team. Destiny was elated to get a nice job without even really looking. There was one issue Destiny really needed a car because she would be transporting marketing materials and samples to several locations. Her Dad came to the rescue. Her Mother was picking her up from work one day. Courtney said, "I need to meet your Dad before we go home." Destiny didn't think anything about it. They pulled into a car dealership on the Southside of Chicago. Her Dad walked out from nowhere. Destiny was thinking what is going on here. Her Dad surprised and said," Congratulations", you now have a 1980 Buick Skylark.

Destiny was walking on air, a Bachelor of Science degree in Business Administration, a new job and now a car. It didn't take long for her world to start to crumble. Her car was 6 years old and it started breaking down on a frequent basis. Destiny couldn't afford to keep fixing it, her paycheck was frequently late and when she addressed the situation with her Manager. She acted like she could care less. Destiny decided that this job was not working for her, so she quit.

Destiny never really had a problem acquiring jobs. Her friend Yvonne had a nice position at a company called National Processing where they process peoples check payments. She didn't even tell Yvonne that she was applying for a position there. She interviewed and got the position of a Data Entry Clerk. Destiny was successful in obtaining the position. Yvonne was still attending Chicago State University and she was a Customer Service Representative. When Yvonne found out she got the position she was happy for her. This position was not what Destiny was looking for, but she needed a job. She worked there the Human Resources Department in a Assistant position. She also worked the front desk. She became really good friends with the Human Resource Director. Her name was Cathy. She was about 6 years older than Destiny. Cathy was about 5'8, had medium brown skin color, attractive and very nice to Destiny. She had relocated to Illinois from Kentucky. She was divorced from an older gentleman, who was about 8 years older than her. Her Ex-husband owned a funeral home back in Kentucky and they had a 6 year old son. She asked Destiny to travel to Louisville, KY to visit her Mom and Destiny agreed. She remained friends with Cathy until she left National Processing.

Destiny was ready to move out of her parents' home, but she still wasn't making enough money to move out on her own. Destiny met a young lady about 3 years older than her named Toni who worked at National Processing with her. She lived with her Mother and she desperately wanted to move out just like Destiny wanted to move out of her parents' house. Destiny enjoyed Toni's company and they would go to parties and other events together. Toni worked another job at Chernin's Shoe Store. She felt Toni would make a great roommate.

One day Toni approached Destiny and told her she had a friend that wanted them to move in with her. The young lady lived in Park Forest in a new Townhouse. Destiny got the address and visited the home. It was beautiful. We would each have our own bedrooms and because the rent would be split 3 ways Toni and Destiny could afford the rent. Destiny agreed to move in with Toni into the townhouse. She was excited to be moving at the age of 24 years old. Destiny was at work one day and Toni walked over to her and she looked very upset. Destiny said, "Are you okay, Toni replied, " No I have bad news." Destiny replied, "What's going on?" The lady Shannon was getting ready to dupe us into moving in with her only to steal our money and leave us stranded in the Townhouse. Destiny didn't know Shannon, but she trusted Toni. Toni knew people who knew Shannon's Dad. He was wealthy and purchased the Townhome for Shannon. He wanted Shannon to pull her own weight. He warned her he was going to put her out if she didn't start paying some rent. Shannon came up with the bright idea to get two roommates to pay her rent. She would pocket the money but still not give it to her Father. She in fact was getting ready to move in with her boyfriend. Destiny was angry!! Destiny shouted, "What kind of person makes up such an elaborate plan to use someone?" Destiny was so happy that Toni stopped her evil plan. Destiny decided to keep saving her money until another opportunity came her way that would allow her to move out of her parents' house.

Destiny still wanted to get another job, so she enlisted the help of a temp agency. She started working for Chemical Bank in a Customer Service position. They liked Destiny's work habits and after two months offered her a permanent position in the collections department. She was making more money, but she still didn't make enough money to move. She hated that position because people would curse her out, hang up or make up lies about when they were going to pay their bill. She tried to be pleasant to her customers but as soon as they found out why she was calling most of the customers lost their mind and acted horrible. She decided to step down from her job at National Processing and ask could she return to the Data Entry position so she could work at night. She just kept stacking her money so she could eventually move. She made up in her mind that she needed one good job in order to be happy with her life.

Courtney received a call from Ed Jr., he was getting married. He dated his girlfriend for 4 years before he proposed to her. Her name was Tina. She was about 2 years younger than Destiny. Destiny met her and thought she was nice, but Tina didn't care for Courtney. Destiny had enough issues with her relationships. She wasn't going to try and figure out what issues Tina and Courtney were having. Tina wanted the wedding to be in Los Angeles, CA. She asked Destiny to be a bridesmaid and she wanted Carrie to sing. Destiny and the rest of the family didn't have to worry about staying in a hotel because Courtney's brother lived in Los Angeles.

The wedding was beautiful, it was sunny and warm. Destiny's dress was beautiful. Destiny was praying she had a decent dress because most bridesmaid's dresses are ugly, but Tina did a great job at picking out some cute dresses. The groomsmen were super handsome and Destiny was being charmed by Ed's friend Maurice. She even got a little kiss from him before she left to go back to Chicago. He had her number and called her for a couple of months.

CHAPTER 4

Moving On Up In The World

————•• ••——————

She wanted to pledge Alpha Kappa Alpha, but the Sorority was suspended for hazing at Chicago State. She knew she had to pledge Graduate Chapter. Destiny was determined to realize her dream to be an AKA. Patty invited her to pledge. She pledged June 1, 1991. Destiny was in a great space. She received a phone call from Patty two weeks later regarding a phenomenal job opportunity. Destiny had always wanted to work at an advertising agency. She watched Bewitched growing up and the main characters husband worked at an advertising agency. Patty told her that she met the head of the Media Department. Her name was Roberta. She also just happened to be her Alpha Kappa Alpha Soror. Destiny went in for an interview. She thought it went well but a month went by and she didn't hear anything. They had offered the position to someone else. Destiny was second on the list because of her typing ability the other candidate typed better. Instead of Destiny feeling defeated she started getting her typing skills up. She never wanted anyone to say she didn't get something because of her deficiencies. The interview was in June and she decided to keep looking for her dream job. While she was at work her Supervisor came to her desk. When she walked over to her desk, she said you have a emergency phone call. Destiny was so nervous, every bad situation popped up in her head. She just knew a family member had died. When she answered the call, it was her Soror Roberta. She said I'm sorry I lied to your Supervisor, she told her that she was Destiny's Sister and there was an emergency going on and she needed to speak to you. Destiny said, "Okay, what's going on?" Roberta asked her if she was still interested in the Media Estimator position in the Media department at BR Advertising Agency? Destiny almost screamed but she realized she was at work. She had to stop and control her emotions which were running rampant. This was her dream job. She instantly knew that moving away from her parents wasn't a distant dream anymore. Soror Roberta said, "Are you still there?" Yes, shouted Destiny. Her Supervisor said, Destiny are you okay?"

Yes, Destiny replied. Roberta asked if she could go to the hospital in order to take her drug tests. Destiny of course said yes. Destiny wandered what happened to the other young lady that got the job. She was using drugs and was fired only after working there for one month.

When she hung up the phone, she was speechless. She couldn't believe that she only had to pass the drug test and the job would be hers. Destiny hated lying but she said that her sister needed her tomorrow. Her supervisor told her she would have to use one of her vacation days. She didn't care because she knew that she was getting her dream. Destiny passed her drug test and reported to work August 5, 1991. She loved this job. She was responsible for Media placement for Newspaper, Radio, Magazines, Television, and Billboards. She met several celebrities, participated in a radio commercial for one of their clients and was wined and dined by several people who needed this agency to advertise their products. Destiny would get all kinds of free tickets. Destiny was talking to Roberta about moving out of her parents' home. Roberta's told Destiny about her Cousin who had just gotten married and was leasing her Condominium. Roberta contacted Roberta's Cousin. She was a very sweet lady named Marcy. Marcy decided that Destiny would be a great fit for the Condo and she agreed to let Destiny live there. It seemed like 1991 was Destiny's year. New job and now new place to live.

Destiny still wasn't making a lot of money, so she asked a friend name Gerri to move in as her roommate. Gerri was frantic to move out of her parents' house as well. Gerri was 25 years old. She was married at the tender age of 19 years old. When she divorced her husband a year prior, she had moved in with her parents along with her 5-year-old daughter. Destiny's parents wanted her to live with them until she got married but marriage seemed to be very far away. Destiny had just broken up with yet another young man. She was ready to give up on love, until she met a nice-looking guy while partying with her roommate and her cousin Dee. His name was Mario.

Mario was not that tall, he was 5'10. Destiny could just hear her Mom's voice talking about how she could date such a short man. Courtney believed any man under 6'0 was short.

Destiny met Mario a week after her Grandmother Alberta passed away. Her Grandfather Oliver had passed away a year prior. They were both 87 years old when they passed away because Her Grandfather was a year older than her Grandmother. Mario was very nice to her and she was in mourning. Destiny let a lot of things slide because she just needed some comfort. Mario was able to sneak into her life for that reason.

Mario stuck to Destiny like glue and she thought it was cute. He actually was planning his next move. He was everything Destiny needed him to be. He did have his own apartment. He didn't have a car which irritated Destiny's soul. Destiny hated when grown men didn't own a car. Mario was so nice to her she let it slide. Destiny was 29 years old and he was 25 years old. Destiny just really wanted to be married by the time she turned 30 years old. They dated for 6 months and Mario walked into her bedroom and sat on her bed. When she turned around, he noticed he had a calendar in his hands. He said, would you marry me when I said yes. He handed me a calendar and Destiny picked July 8, 1993. Her Grandmothers always wanted her to find a good man. Destiny had no idea that this man was not a good man at all!!

Destiny wanted a huge wedding. This wedding was getting out of control. Her grandmother had left her Mom some money so Courtney was ready, willing, and able to spend, spend and spend some more on her daughter's wedding. She was going to be married at her childhood church, her Mother was a musician, so she hired a string quartet for the wedding. Destiny had almost 300 guests attending her wedding reception. The grand total was $10,000 which was high for a wedding and reception in 1993. Destiny's Dad ask Courtney, "How is the wedding planning going for your wedding?" When Courtney told Destiny what her Dad said she started laughing. Courtney was able to have any input on Edmond Jr.'s wedding, so she loved being able to help Destiny plan her wedding. Destiny loved her Mom helping her because Courtney was classy and had impeccable taste.

Destiny had now been at her job for 2 years and was promoted to Media Assistant. Her director told her she had a great chance of receiving a raise.

A young man started visiting the office. HIs name was Barack Obama. All the ladies thought that he was attractive. He was single. He was with an African American Mayoral candidate. The City of Chicago wanted another Mayor like Mayor Harold Washington. Mr. Obama seemed to be very interested in being mentored by this Mayoral candidate. The office was buzzing about him marrying a young lady named Michelle. Destiny wasn't high ranking enough to get an invitation to his wedding. Her director received an invitation but didn't attend the nuptials.

Destiny's big day was finally here. The wedding of the century. Destiny was starting to have doubts. She went on with the wedding anyway. This was by far the worst mistake Destiny would ever make. The ceremony was beautiful. The wedding had beautiful music and the singing was impeccable. Destiny looked beautiful. She had 6 Brides Maids, 6 Grooms Men two Flower Girls and a Ring Bearer. The String Quartet was very nice. The Bride and Groom went to Las Vegas for their Honeymoon the next day.

CHAPTER 5

The End of Marriage No. 1

--•-•-••-

Her Director who mentored her quit leaving a gigantic void at the agency. Destiny was so sad that Roberta was leaving because of some issues she had with the President of the company. One of the employees of our department was terminated and she tried to sue the company. Destiny didn't know all the background information, but it seemed like the President blamed the Director for the lawsuit. The only thing the terminated employee received was unemployment. The lawsuit was dropped for not having any merit.

Her director left in the middle of negotiations for Destiny's raise. Her new boss was a total pain in the butt. When the new director arrived, she demanded she be a Vice President. Her name was Nina. She was from New York and had the worse personality in the world. She bragged about being a pioneer for African American woman in advertising. I commend anyone for being a pioneer, but did the whole agency have to hear about it every day? She acted like a total Diva. This woman's attitude was beyond horrible. The workday started at 9:00 am. She never adhered to being on time. The former Director was always there working, but Nina waltzed in whenever she felt like it. She would come at 10:00am, 11:00 am or 12 noon she didn't care. She would be too busy getting her hair and nails done. Destiny had a personality like both of her parents, which meant she didn't put up with foolishness no matter who you were. She asked Destiny to let her know when she was leaving. Destiny told her "If you look at the clock and it is 5:00pm then you know I am leaving. Nina was trying to make Destiny work overtime for no good reason just because she didn't get to work in a timely manner.

Destiny grew tired of this crazy woman. Destiny knew she was up for a raise, so she concentrated on receiving her raise. She worked very hard and knew she deserved the raise. Nina came to her desk and said, "You have received a raise, but the President of the company didn't give you the amount you wanted. Destiny was so disappointed, but she had a bad feeling that Nina was lying to her. One day while Nina was out at a meeting. She looked for her file. When she opened her file, she discovered that Nina never asked the President for the amount Destiny and the former Director talked about. She changed the amount and submitted that amount. Destiny could only surmise that Nina was trying to look like she was saving the company some money. Destiny realized that she couldn't work for a dishonest person. She began looking for another job.

Destiny's marriage of 2 years was also not working out. Mario was a closet alcoholic. He also smoked. He never smoked in front of Destiny before that got married. Destiny's Dad was an alcoholic and a smoker and her Dad ruined his health. Destiny saw all the things her Mom went through. She didn't want to go through the same things her Mom dealt with involving her Dad. Her Mom was constantly rushing her Dad to the emergency room because of his bad habits. She tried to talk to Mario about getting help for his drinking, but he started avoiding her by coming home late from work and going out with his friends. She noticed he also started lying about everything. His lies were so ludicrous only a moron would believe him. He called Destiny early one morning about 4am. He said the reason he wasn't at home is because he was in an accident and the car flipped over. Destiny replied, "Oh your car flipped over but you're okay?" Mario said, "Yes it flipped back over and now I'm at my friend's garage and he is fixing it. Destiny was being very condescending and said, "So it flipped over and you were able to drive it, really? Destiny said she would speak with him later. She knew he was lying. He wasn't even good at lying. She prayed about her situation and God gave her instructions on what to with her marriage. The best thing in her life was her relationship with God.

Destiny was ready to move out of the Condo into a home. She was ready to be a homeowner and Mario agreed. Destiny wanted to save her marriage and Mario wanted to try as well. She felt like following the plan God set for her would guide her on what next steps to make with her relationship with Mario. She always believed that obedience was better than sacrifice. She was glad she was being obedient to God's will for her life. She wasn't always obedient to God's word and her disobedience always caused her issues. She talked to Mario about moving in with her parents because then they could save their money. He said yes even though she could tell he really didn't want to move in with them. They moved out of the Condo and moved in with her Mom and Dad.

This was one of the best decision Destiny would ever make. Mario could no longer sneak out, get drunk and hang out at all hours with his friends. He felt he was under a microscope and he hated it. They weren't ready to move out, but Destiny knew Mario was unhappy. Destiny contacted a Realtor and they started looking at houses. One Saturday when Destiny was at her parents' house. She received a call from Mario. He was calling from work and was distraught, Destiny wandered what was wrong with him. He said, "Change the sheets on the bed immediately". She wondered why and asked him. He told her he had the sexually transmitted disease Crabs. Crabs is slang for pubic lice. Destiny knew she didn't have this disease. She asked him how he contracted it, he replied a toilet seat. Destiny knew he was lying. This was the last straw. She demanded that he go straight to the doctor and be tested for sexually transmitted diseases. She knew he was embarrassed, but her health was important to her. She knew he was cheating on her but his was totally out of control. Destiny was now worried for her life. She knew he was cheating on her, but she would discover that the cheating was far worse than she could have ever imagined. She didn't want to contract AIDS or any other sexually transmitted disease. Destiny was not about to let a man kill her or infect her. When he came home from work, he turned everything around on her. He stated he was not happy and he was tired of living with her parents and had the nerve to give her a ultimatum. Destiny was appalled that he told her if they didn't move, he was moving. He then turned around and left her parents' house for good.

Destiny knew this was all a smoke screen for everything he was doing wrong in the marriage. Mario refused to tell her where he was living. She called his older brother and he was there. His brother told him that he needed to go back home and work things out with her. Mario called Destiny and asked her was she ready to move into their new home yet. She thought to herself this man is totally dodging the issues in their marriage. Since Mario wasn't going to be honest about his breakdown in the marriage Destiny started to do her own investigation. Seek and you shall find was her motto which came from the bible. Her friend Marie called her with some very interesting information. Mario was responsible for getting her husband a job at his place of employment. They worked at a delivery service and they were drivers. Her husband told her one day they met these two women and Mario started dating her. She is the one that gave him Crabs. He later broke up with her for giving him Crabs. Mario was in a relationship with another woman while being married to Destiny. When Marie told her this information, she wasn't surprised. Marie just gave her more history to this jaded story of her turbulent marriage.

Once Destiny asked for God's help the misguided deeds of Mario kept unfolding. Destiny still didn't know where he was living. The one good habit Mario had was handing over is check to her so she could pay bills. Destiny knew he had given her most of his money. She knew he had to be living with someone because he didn't have any credit cards and she had most of his money. Her Sister also still lived with their parents. Carrie was now using Destiny's old phone from when she previously lived there. When her Grandmother Alberta lived in the house, she used that same phone. Carrie was paying the phone bill. She noticed some phone numbers that didn't look familiar. The phone bill was itemized and the out of town numbers stuck out like a sore thumb. There were two numbers that kept appearing on her phone bill that she didn't make. Carrie showed Destiny the phone bill and said maybe this will help you find out where Mario is living. Mario worked in Gary, Indiana the phone numbers were Indiana numbers. Destiny lived in the South Suburbs of Illinois she figured that he was living with someone in Indiana.

Destiny was nervous because she knew the truth about Mario's whereabouts were getting ready to be uncovered. She dialed the first number and it was a hospital in Indiana. She put a pin on the first phone number and moved on to the next number. A little girl answered the phone Destiny said, "May I speak to Mario?" The little girl said, "Hold on." Destiny could hear the conversation going on in the background. She heard Mario say, "Who is it?" The Little girl came back to the phone and said, "Who is this"? Destiny said, "Tell him it's his wife." He came to the phone and Destiny stared asking him where he was. As usual he started lying saying that he was staying in a lady's house he just met. Destiny busted him out and asked him what woman is going to let you stay in her house rent free. She told him she knew he was in a relationship with her. He kept denying it.

Mario had been gone for 6 months. Destiny considered the marriage to be over, so she sought out a divorce attorney. Her parents loaned her the $1,000 she needed to end her marriage. Destiny was sitting at home one day when the phone rang it was Mario's new Girlfriend. She revealed a lot about their relationship while talking on the phone. Her name was Renee. Renee was 42 years old and Mario was 27 years old. She had two children a 11-year-old daughter and a 22-year-old son. Mario was 5 years older than his Girlfriends son. She told Destiny she doesn't usually get involved in other people's issues, but she noticed he never had any money after working 5 days for 8 hours. When she questioned him about it, he said he was giving it to his Ex-wife. She couldn't understand why he was giving money to his Ex-wife. Destiny said, "So you think I'm his Ex-wife?" She said, "Yes". Destiny told her that they were still married when they started dating. Destiny asked her how they met. Renee said they met in a Wal-Mart. Mario told her he had been divorced for 2 years and that he was looking to move to Indiana because he worked in Gary, IN. He asked her for her number and they have been together for 8 months. Destiny was past upset. He started dating her before they even broke up. Renee said she would never be the other woman. She claimed that she was a Christian and that her ex-husband cheated on her and she would never do that to anyone. I told her we were separated now and she could have him. When Destiny hung up the phone, she made an appointment to go pay her lawyer so she could start the divorce process. Mario was served his divorce papers at work. Marie's husband was there when it happened. He told Marie that Mario was really embarrassed when they served him. Mario was also angry with Destiny for embarrassing him at work. When Marie told Destiny that she couldn't believe his selfishness. He abandoned the marriage, cheated on her with several women, and contracted a sexual disease and he is angry at her. Destiny was unbothered by his total lack of respect for her.

Mario never showed up to any of the court dates. The final court date he was also a no show. He never wanted a divorce. He just wanted Destiny to put up with his philandering ways. Destiny noticed that God instructing her to move in with her parents actually smoked Mario out. He felt too many eyes on him. He was angry that he was being held to a standard. He bailed on the relationship because he was a coward. The Attorney was able to get the divorce without his signature. It was obvious that he received every notice because they were sent to his place of employment.

Destiny was now divorced. She was 32 years old and sad that she still didn't have any children. She thought since you didn't get pregnant, that she may have some issues. She went to the doctor to find out if she was okay. She discovered she had a tilted uterus. This was a condition that she inherited from her Dad's side of the family. She dated a few guys but nothing serious. She decided to concentrate on her job. She still was working for a maniac of a boss and this was the year to dump her spouse and her boss. One down and one to go!

Destiny contacted a Hair company Lee's Products that was started by an African American Businessman in 1965. She interviewed to work in their Media department. She waited for two days and they hired her. She gave a 2 week notice and went to work for the new company. Everyone was nice to Destiny. This company was a lot smaller than what she was use to the pay was better but she missed her old advertising agency. Her new Director was a little weird, but she liked Karla. They were the only ones in the media department. In her last job there were 3 other people plus her. She worked there 2 years and it was pleasant, but Destiny felt she wanted more. Karla was a great mentor and Destiny learned a lot from her about the Beauty industry and the media industry.

Karla called Destiny into her office. She told her to close the door. Destiny thought, "I hope I'm not getting fired"! Karla told her she was leaving. She was going back to work at another advertising agency she worked at before she joined Lee's company. Destiny thought they were the dynamic duo. She wandered what she would do after she left. Since Karla was an executive she had to give a 4 week notice. In the meantime, Destiny applied for her position. The Marketing Director already had someone in mind for the position. The problem was beside the owners Karla and Destiny were the only ones that knew the department forwards and backwards. When the new Media Director arrived, Destiny trained her. Michelle was a nice lady, but Destiny was tired of being looked over. While Karla was there, she took some of Destiny's ideas as her own. She was not having it anymore. She was ready to move on again, because there were no other promotions she was interested in at that company.

Destiny decided to bide her time at Lee's Products until she could secure another good position. Destiny decided to try her hand at romance again. She used the personal ads and met a retired NFL player. His name was Steve. Steve played for the New Orleans Saints years before they met. Steve told Destiny he was 5 years older than her. She later found out he was 10 years older than her. Steve acted like he was her Prince Charming. He was 6'3, handsome, light skin and curly hair. Destiny thought he was too old for her, but her sister told her to give him a chance.

Steve was another guy who presented himself as a person he wasn't. Destiny actually wanted to take it slow. She didn't want to be married 7 times like her famous Aunt Diana. She didn't even want to be married 3 times like her maternal grandmother Alberta. When Steve met Destiny, he told her she looked sad. She was sad but with her faith in God she prayed everything would eventually work out. Destiny's Dad grew up very poor and he had to navigate his way through gangs and criminal activities. He always worked and wanted to do things the right way. He didn't trust Steve. He saw him as a street wise guy. Destiny thought her Dad was going overboard as usual. She would find out her Dad's instincts were right.

Destiny felt like she was just along for the ride in her relationship with Steve. Steve was defiantly an Alpha male. He tried to be there for Destiny whenever she had issues. Her car broke down, so he gave his 1992 Cadillac Deville to her. Destiny was grateful even though the car was 4 years old, but she didn't have a car note and that worked for her. She asked him for the title, but he kept saying he was going to give it to her, but he never did. Destiny decided he was trying to control her, so she decided to go buy herself another car. She decided on purchasing the 1994 Buick Regal, she got a good deal because the car was 2 years old. When Steve found out he was less than pleased. Destiny let him know she was a no-nonsense person when it came to something's. She knew he had no intentions of giving her the title to his car. She hated a liar, or people who volunteered a lie. She never asked him to give her a car. If Steve changed his mind he should have said so!!

Steve noticed Destiny was being a little cold to him. They had been dating about 10 months. He was married once and so was she. He decided he didn't want her to leave him, so he proposed to her. He took her to dinner then to Jewelers row downtown. She thought he was buying a ring for himself. He proposed to her once they walked inside the jewelry store.

Destiny said yes to his proposal. He wanted her to create the perfect ring. She actually had the ring designed exactly the way she wanted it to be. The ring was gorgeous, it was a princess cut 4 carat diamond ring. Destiny wasn't in love with Steve, but he loved her and that was good enough for her. It took 4 months to get the ring because he gave it to her for her birthday, which was June 5th.

Destiny was ready to leave Lee's Products. She was doing most of the work but not being recognized for her efforts. Destiny heard through the grapevine that the old President of the BR Agency took over the reins of another Hair Care Company called Sheen Hair Company. Carol's brother had started his own company, so he stepped down as the President of the company. She contacted Carol Sheen to ask for a job. Carol was elated that Destiny wanted to come back to work for her. She never wanted her to leave the Advertising Agency. She just couldn't deal with her ex-boss from hell.

Carol created a Territory Merchandising position for Destiny. She set Destiny up with an interview. Destiny went in for the interview which was basically just a formality. She was so excited that during the interview one of Carol's executives told her she had the position and report to Human Resources. Her start date was November 11, 1996. This position came with so many bells and whistles: She had full medical, a monthly stipend to pay her car note, an expense account, she was able to expense her gas, and she also received $350 with her first paycheck. This money was given to her in case she needed to travel out of town. Destiny loved this job. She worked in the field. She never like working inside of an office because she felt that she would be micromanaged. Destiny hated that. She hated to be micromanaged, when she worked inside of an office that is what most managers did to her. She always did her job, there was no need to hover over her.

Destiny thought she had it all a Fiancé the loved her a great position and she had even joined a recording choir that traveled all over the world to sing. Destiny was always scared that something would go wrong after all it always did and she was always waiting for the other shoe to drop. The other shoe did drop and boy did it drop!! Destiny was always a dreamer.

She had a prophetic gift. She would also have visions that came true. She prayed about her upcoming nuptials. The minute she sought the Lord's blessing on her marriage she was barraged with horrible nightmares and visions. She decided to seek wise counsel from her Pastor.

Destiny had not contacted her Pastor yet. She was sitting at home watching television when the phone rang. It was her Pastor. Pastor Daniel Harris called her. This man was an extraordinary preacher and had a great prophetic anointing on his life. He preached about things that Destiny wouldn't hear from anyone else until 15 to 20 years later. He was absolutely ahead of his time. He said that God had put me on his heart. She was dumbfounded and couldn't believe that God cared about her that much. Destiny said, what's up? He asked her if she was still engaged to Steve. Destiny replied that she was still engaged. He said she needed to continue to pray for God to show her his true feelings and motives. He said that God had revealed some character flaws in Steve and that she needed to be careful.

The phone call from Pastor Harris really unhinged her. She started to pray and ask God to show her Steve's character flaws. Destiny felt like she let the flood gates open because her prayers were being answered. The very next day a lady called her and told her she was his girlfriend. Steve had been driving a brand new 1996 Mercedes Benz Class SL 500. The lady on the phone said it was her car. Destiny had only seen the car a couple of times because Steve kept it in the garage. The first time Destiny saw it was when Steve picked her up at the airport. She verified a lot of information on him, so she knew that she was in his life and knew him extremely well. Destiny wanted to verify some information on him, so she asked her. He told Destiny he had 2 kids and he really had 5. Destiny called Steve's Mom to confirm what his so-called girlfriend told her. She asked her about the lady who called her. She knew her but she said they broke up and she just will not let go of Steve. Destiny asked if the Mercedes Benz Class SL 500 was his car his Mom said no. His Mom knew it was the stalker ex-girlfriend's car in fact she told Steve to stop driving this woman's car because she knew the lady was a little unhinged. Destiny confirmed the amount of kids he had with his Mom.

He in fact had 5 kids and not just 2 kids. Destiny was annoyed at her Fiancé and his lies. When she confronted him about his lies, he said he didn't want to turn her off by telling her he had 5 kids, since she didn't have any. Destiny couldn't believe he would deny his children just to be in a relationship with her. She thought to herself, who does that? Destiny was turned off about the lies he told.

Destiny needed a break from Steve. She asked her Mom to take a trip with her to Minnesota to the Mall of America. Her Mom started telling her that Edmond told her he was doing business with a drug dealer. Her Dad stumbled on the information by mistake. When she heard this, she was done with him. Courtney said Destiny's engagement ring was beautiful, but she felt it was something off about it. She wanted to go to a jeweler and get the real value for her ring. Destiny knew he had the ring created for her, so she literally ran into the jeweler to show off her beautiful ring. She took off the ring and waited for the jeweler to give Courtney the good news. He said the stones surrounding the princess cut diamond were real and they were about 2 carets, then drum roll please, the big diamond was a cubic zirconium. She was flabbergasted. How could this man perpetrate such a huge fraud? Destiny was a drama queen. Her Mother caught her because she almost fainted. She knew that this was the end of their relationship.

The next day they flew back to Chicago. Steve picked them up from the airport and Destiny was looking at him like he was the most despicable creature on the planet. They dropped her Mom off and then Steve asked Destiny why she was so quiet. She then unleashed some words that were not so nice, she said, "How the hell are you going to give me half a fake ring?" She went on the say, "Anyone can tell you were trying to perpetrate a fraud because some of the engagement ring was real and some of it was fake." He immediately tried to deflect by saying, "I was not going to have you working in the field with a real ring." He also added, "Why did you feel the need to see if the ring was real? Destiny said, "Really it's my fault now that you purchased a fake ring for me?" Destiny told him that her Mother never thought the ring was real. Destiny wanted to prove her Mom wrong instead she was totally embarrassed. She told Steve she stuck up for him and ran into the jewelry store to prove her wrong. Steve started calling her Mother Ghetto and ignorant. No one has ever called her intelligent Mother Ghetto. Destiny dropped a bomb on him and said, we are over!! She got out of his car and took her suitcase and walked in the house. He sped off in his car.

Steve kept calling her and leaving nasty messages on her answering machine. He talked about her Sister and her Mother. When they had nothing to do with him and his crazy lying ways. Steve called her one day and she had enough of him leaving nasty messages on her answering machine. She started blasting him by say "You run over shoe wearing, deceitful liar, how dare you talk about my family members? "Do me a favor and lose my phone number period!" This is the end of our conversation forever!" She also added, "You are a broke, no good piece of crap, enjoy your life without me in it."

Destiny decided she needed a distraction. She was back on the personals. She dated an Entrepreneur who was still in love with his son's Mother. Destiny never met a guy who constantly showed pictures of his child's Mother. She was amazed at when she asked him could she see a picture of his son they all had the child's Mother in them. She told him that wasn't a wise move to keep showing pictures of the child's Mother. She told him that they he may possibly still be in love with her because he talked about her endlessly. She decided to bow out gracefully. She knew she couldn't compete with the love this man had for his son's mother. She asked him to lose her phone number as well. Destiny just started hanging out with friends and family and enjoying her job.

CHAPTER 6

Moving On To Number 2

••●●••

D estiny was a person who should never be bored. She would often get in trouble because of boredom. She was sitting at home one day and behold she was bored out of her mind. She picked up the phone and called her friend Yvonne. Yvonne was a Single Mom who was looking for Mr. Right or Mr. Right now, as well. They decided to hit a neighborhood bar called Reggie's Bar in Blue Island, IL, even though older men frequented this bar the young ladies didn't mind. They were both 33 years old and they were both ready to be around some mature gentlemen 40 and over. This spot was perfect for two young ladies who were doing well in every facet of their lives except their love lives. They would usually sit at a table talking and the waitress would point and say those gentlemen want to buy you a drink. We would say yes and thank them. What the ladies really like was that sometime the men would leave and not even come over and then other times they would ask could they join them. Some of the Blue Island Firemen would join us. We were never pressured to sleep with anybody because they purchased a drink for us.

Destiny started inviting other friends and family to Reggie's Bar, it was a hole in the wall, but they always had a good time. The Disc Jockey was always good. They had a good time dancing with the guys who frequented the bar. Destiny and Yvonne were there one Friday night and they both saw the most gorgeous guy in the universe. He was tall 6'4, dark brown skin color, hazel eyes, buff and handsome. He was defiantly tall, dark and oh so handsome! He had on a muscle shirt and they could tell he had a six pack. He was thin but he had muscles. Destiny didn't really like thin guys because since she was thin and she felt a thin guy couldn't protect her. This thinking was dumb because even when men were thin. They still had brute strength. He looked our age, which they weren't use too. They had gotten so use to older men they almost forgot a guy their age frequented the bar. He walked over to the table and asked if he could sit down of course the ladies said yes. Yvonne had her eye on another guy, so she excused herself and walked over to the bar where her guy was sitting.

He introduced himself. His name was Daniel Hardwick. He asked Destiny her name and she just stared at him like a star struck teenager. He said, excuse me did you hear me? Destiny snapped out of it and told him her name. He asked her what she was drinking. She told him Malibu and Pineapple Juice and then he went to the bar and ordered their drinks. They talked until 3:00am. They talked about their families and his 8-year-old son. They exchanged phone numbers. He presented himself as a great guy, but Destiny knew only time would tell.

Daniel was an electrician and he made a very good living. He was raised in Chicago but had moved to Michigan City when his Grandmother became ill. He stayed there once she died. He would write Destiny, send her cards and gifts through the mail. If he wasn't visiting her over the weekend, she was visiting him. Destiny needed this distraction because Steve was still calling her. She was happy she could leave town and not have to be bothered with Steve. Daniel had never been married and wanted to get married. Destiny was a little gun shy about getting married. She really only wanted to get married again because she didn't want a child born out of wedlock. Her Mother would never let her live it down if she wasn't married when she had a baby. Daniel was a little turned off that she wasn't frantic about getting married again. She had a horrible first marriage and just broke up with her fiancé. Daniel was working 2 full time jobs and he wanted to see Destiny, but he was too tired to drive to Country Club Hills, IL to see her. She decided since it was Friday and she didn't have to go to work she would drive out to Michigan City, IN. He had a big house with 5 bedrooms. I slept in a separate room. He was nice regarding her trying to wait until she was married again before she had sex. She noticed he was very irritable, so she tried to lower his stress by giving him a massage. He wanted to go out and Destiny agreed. He wanted some junk food from the store. Destiny was always down for junk food. When he got out the car he ran into some friends. They talked a few minutes then he went into the store. When he got in the car, he missed some of the items she wanted when she pointed out his mistakes. He exploded on her and told her he hated her. She was traumatized by his behavior. She told him to take her to his house. She packed up her stuff and left. She refused to be emotionally or verbally abused by any man.

The verbal assault from Daniel was in August. Destiny ignored his phone calls for a month. She decided to pick up the phone at the end of September. He said he missed her and he apologized profusely. She accepted his apology but defiantly did not trust this man. Daniel was so happy that not only did Destiny accept his apology, but she took him back. They decided to start over again and not talk about what happened in the past. It was December and the relationship were going great. He asked her to get dressed up because he had a surprise for her. He took her to an elegant restaurant. They were escorted to a room that was decorated beautifully. Destiny felt special because they were the only ones in this room. She didn't know Daniel arranged everything. He got on his knees and proposed to Destiny, she was shocked, but she said yes!!!

She couldn't wait to tell her Mother, Father, Brother and Sister. She asked Daniel if he had spoken with her Dad and he said yes. Her Dad never let on that he had spoken with Daniel. Her Mother and Sister didn't really like Daniel. They both said they couldn't put their finger on it but something about him was off. Her Dad saw him as a hardworking man and he thought he would make a great provider for Destiny. Destiny was worried about Daniel she hadn't spoken to him in a while. Destiny was talking to her friend Carla from church about him disappearing. She said that she had prayed if he wasn't any good, he would vanish. Destiny thought she was joking at first. Her friend assured her she was not joking. Carla obviously felt there was something off about him. Destiny was a little disturbed by what her friend Carla said, so she decided to get to the bottom of why she felt the way she did about Daniel, Carla really didn't want to tell Destiny but she finally said, "It is something about him that I find very dark." Destiny was really confused now. She never thought of him as being dark like the Devil. Destiny was more than just religious, she felt like she was more spiritual. She felt she had a relationship with God. Why she was not seeing the darkness, she asked herself.

Destiny found a piece of paper that Daniel had written his Sister Susan's phone number on. She decided to call the number. When Susan answered she introduced herself. She told Susan they were engaged. She was worried about him because she hadn't heard from him in 2 weeks and that was not like him. Susan was starting to worry because she hadn't heard from him either. Susan did tell Destiny that this isn't the first time Daniel has pulled a disappearing act. He disappears from time to time and then shows back up like nothing has happened. Destiny's phone rang it was about a week before Valentines' day when she answered she heard a familiar voice it was Daniel calling like nothing was wrong. He did admit that he was feeling a little nervous about getting married. Destiny was surprised because he was the one pushing the whole marriage agenda. He profusely apologized for being nervous about their future.

Daniel wanted to be married before Valentine's Day. Destiny couldn't keep up with him at first. He was nervous now he was rushing her. He always knew how to get her on his side. They ended up going to the Markham Courthouse on Markham, IL. They decided to get married before Valentines' Day. They got married February 11th. They told their families about 2 days before it happened. Destiny planned on having a vow renewal ceremony for their friends and family in May on the Memorial Day weekend. The ceremony was short and sweet. They went out to dinner after the ceremony. They came home and consummated the marriage. They planned to go to Las Vegas for their honeymoon.

Destiny started feeling queasy. She thought she might just have the stomach flu. She chewed on 2 Tums then she drank some Ginger Ale. Her stomach just wouldn't stop hurting. She was talking to her cousin who had 4 kids and she told her she maybe pregnant. She thought I haven't been married that long. Her Cousin Dee said, "You know it only takes one time, right?" Destiny shouted, "Of course I know that, but I don't think I'm pregnant, but I will go to the doctor." Destiny was 34 years old and she wanted to be a Mom really bad. Destiny was so nervous when she walked into the exam room. When

Destiny's examination was finished the Doctor left the room. It seemed like an eternity for her while the Doctor was gone. When the Doctor stepped back in, he told her congratulations she was pregnant. She almost fainted. She couldn't wait to leave and tell everyone she knew. She told her husband first. She called her Mom at work and told her and then she told her Sister Carrie. Her Mom told her Dad and he was very happy.

Destiny determined she more than likely got pregnant on Valentine's Day. She knew that she wouldn't be too big when she and Daniel did their vow renewal ceremony. The ceremony was performed by her cousin Raymond. Her uncle Rob and his wife Betty let her have the wedding ceremony and reception at his spacious Mansion in Tinley Park IL. Rob and his wife Betty paid for all the food and drinks at the Wedding ceremony. Destiny and Daniel were so grateful because they had started saving for a home of their own. They were living in Destiny's old townhouse she had sold to her sister Carrie. Carrie was sweet to allow them to stay there but they needed to move especially with baby on the way. Daniel decided to sell his home in Michigan City, IN. When the house sold, they would be able to move into an Upper Middle-class neighborhood like her parents lived in. They both had great jobs and Destiny was getting better at saving her money. When she was in her twenty's she didn't care about paying her bills, she later learned that a great credit score and money saved in the bank was much better than the next new outfit. She also hated creditors calling her house. She would do anything for them not to call her ever again in life.

CHAPTER 7

And Baby Makes Three

—•◦•—

Daniel asked Destiny to sit down he wanted to talk to her. He wanted to warn her about his family. Daniel's mother and sister had the same name Susan. Daniel told Destiny that he loved his Mother, but she was a troublemaker. She had only met his Mother briefly, but she didn't seem like a bad person. Destiny liked both his sisters and his brother. His brother Marko had the sweetest wife. Her name was Denise. They bonded the first time they met. She would talk to Destiny's stomach and tell the baby he or she was loved. The whole family tried to turn her against Denise. They said she was territorial and she didn't want them around her husband. They almost talked me into hating her. The moment Destiny walked into her house she made her feel welcome.

Destiny had no idea how truly evil Daniel's family really was. As the months went on Destiny grew closer to Denise.

Denise had 3 children: an older son Deon, he was 12 years old a daughter she was 9 years old and a baby that was 5 months old. Daniel's Mom was going to be moving to South Carolina with her new husband. She had gotten married a year before Destiny and Daniel were married. He was a Pastor. He was not very handsome, but he was extremely nice. He was retiring from his church. He loved Susan a lot. She never really cared for him. She just wanted to see how much money she could get from him. He exaggerated about his home in South Carolina. He told Susan he lived in a 6-bedroom home. She couldn't wait to move and see her new home. Denise was happy she would be moving because she often barged into their house without any notice. She would then eat them out of house and home. Susan wouldn't ask Mario and Denise if she could spend night, she would tell them she was spending the night. Susan was super rude and had no manners.

Destiny grew closer to Denise and further away from the rest of Daniel's family. Daniel's Mom moved with her husband only to return for a visit 2 months later. She told Destiny that her husband had bamboozled her. She asked

Susan what happened. She said the house he told her about only had 4 bedrooms and it was old and run down. Destiny asked her why she needed a 6-bedroom house. Her husband didn't have any children and her children were grown. Susan told Destiny she can't stand a liar. That is why she was upset with her husband. Susan told her husband that if wanted to be with her he would have to sell that house and buy her a newer house. Susan stayed with one of her Sister's Alfreda. Destiny actually liked Alfreda and her husband Joey, but she still didn't really trust them either. Destiny believed in what the bible said, "If possible, so far as it depends on you be at peace with all men." Romans 12:18. As a believer Destiny wanted live peaceably with all people especially her In-laws. She really tried to love her neighbors and relatives. This family really put her love to the test! Susan didn't have a job, since she had run away from her husband. She was broke. Daniel's Sister Susan called and said their Mom needed some money. Daniel and Destiny discussed everything. Destiny didn't have a problem with giving his Mom money, but they weren't wealthy. His Mother needed to either get a job or go back to her husband.

Destiny noticed that Daniel was insulted by her statements regarding his Mom. She said she loved his Mom, but they couldn't afford to take care of her. Daniel's family didn't follow many bible principles, one being the man should cleave to his wife. They acted like In-laws were Outlaws. Denise tried to tell Destiny how Daniel's family was, but Destiny always wanted to give everyone a fair chance. She never wanted to judge anyone. Destiny finally saw everything that Denise said was the truth. Destiny and Denise developed an allegiance against Daniel's family. The battle lines were drawn. They started showing Destiny they hated her as much as they hated Denise. They never claimed to be Christians, but Daniel said he was a Christian. He did try to protect her from his family but Destiny worried that he may not be able keep taking up for her because he had a close relationship with them. Destiny's hormones were all over the place. Daniel tried to be careful when talking to her. He knew that she was fragile because of the pregnancy.

Destiny looked great. She was worried that since she was a little older than most first time Mom's she wouldn't navigate this pregnancy very well. She did have morning sickness for 3 months, but she was fine her 4th month. Daniel was the perfect husband. She didn't know how women without spouses could deal with such an emotional time without any support. Her dreams were coming true. A nice handsome husband, a baby on the way and a church home she loved.

Daniel told his wife that as soon as she delivered the baby. They would move out of her townhouse into his mother's old condominium on the lake front. His mother had gotten a very good deal on the condo. Her husband paid it off for her. Destiny didn't know this information until she was getting ready to deliver the baby. She wandered why his mom never mentioned still having the condo. Destiny would never understand this woman. Why was she staying with other family members if she had a whole condo that was paid for? The confusion was real for Destiny. She did something she always did and called Denise. When Denise answered she said, I'm so glad you answered the phone!" Denise asked her, "What's going on?" Destiny told her the whole conversation she had with her husband about Susan having a condo that she didn't know about. Denise knew about but the condo, but she didn't know she still had it. She thought Susan sold it.

Destiny's baby was due at the end of October or beginning of November. She was super excited about her new baby. Destiny and Daniel didn't know the sex of their baby and Destiny didn't care she just wanted a healthy baby. Daniel had a son already, so he wanted a girl. Daniel started packaging their belongings up for their big move. Destiny's feet were swollen but she only had one more month to go. Her stomach was small for about 6 months. People didn't even know she was pregnant. Her belly got a little bigger than seemed to explode the last month of her pregnancy. The week before she was to give birth. She became very ill. She had to be rushed to the hospital. She couldn't keep down anything not even liquids. Daniel couldn't stay with her because he had just started a new job. He missed one day because he was worried about his wife. When she was released from the hospital, she begged her husband to go to work. Her sister was a teacher, her parents were still working. They were in education. Her Mom was a high school counselor and her Dad was a teacher at an Elementary School. He also owed a construction business. They promised to check in on Destiny when they got off of work.

Destiny was asleep upstairs in her townhouse when she heard the doorbell ringing. Her parents had come to check on her. She heard them outside screaming her name. She must have slept through the doorbell ringing, so they became concerned. She ran downstairs to open the door for them. She was so embarrassed. She hoped her neighbors didn't hear them outside screaming her name. When she opened the door, her parents were frantic with worry. Destiny told her parents to calm down and that she was fine. Her parents were glad that their daughter was fine.

On November 3, 1998 Destiny became very ill. She had a doctor's appointment, so she waited for her 5:00pm appointment. She had been communicating with her husband and Mother all day. Her Mother asked if she could come to her appointment with her. Destiny said her Mom was welcome to come. Destiny's Mom was very outspoken and did not have any limits on what she said to anyone. Courtney asked the doctor when he thought the baby would arrive. It was Tuesday November 3rd, the doctor believed she would deliver her baby on Thursday or Friday. Destiny was hooked to a fetal monitor. The baby was doing okay and was not in any distress. Courtney pointed out that her daughter was in distress because she had not eaten in 4 days by the time the baby comes it will be 6 days. Courtney was very upset her daughter couldn't keep any food or liquid down. She would vomit all day long. The doctor said if this continues, he will put in an IV for her to get her nutritional health. The doctor sent Destiny home. When Destiny arrived home, she sat on the couch and fell asleep. She was asleep for about 2 hours and then these extreme labor pains woke her up. She dealt with it for about 4 hours. Then she went upstairs and told her husband. He asked her how far the labor pains were. She said there were about 10 minutes. He said he would get dressed so they could go. She went downstairs and noticed it was taking Daniel a long time to come downstairs, so she went back upstairs. She screamed, "Daniel are you sleep, really?" He woke up and finished getting ready.

Destiny was on her way to the Olympia Fields Osteopathic Hospital at 3:00am. She was having the worst labor pains ever. Luckily, they only lived about 8 minutes away from the hospital. The nurse checked her in and she was taken to the birthing room. This room had a 46-inch color television in the room. The nurse came in and said that they were going to send me home because I was not ready yet. Destiny was laying in the bed and her water broke. The nurse came in the room and Destiny told her that her water broke. The nurse replied, "You can't go home now you will be having your baby soon.

Destiny needed to call her Mom and Dad to let them know she was at the hospital. She knew Daniel was calling his immediate family on his cell phone because he left the room. Destiny woke her Mom up. Courtney said, you're not having that baby until after I get off from work. I'll see you after I get off work. There was no trying to convince Courtney that the baby was coming sooner than they thought. She called her sister Carrie. Carrie was upset that they didn't wake her up so she could have come to the hospital. Carrie told Destiny she would be there after work. Destiny thought to herself why does my family make everything about them? Destiny asked the nurse had she seen her husband. The nurse told her he went to the car to get his camera. Destiny begged the nurse to give her something because the labor pains had increased. She told her that she didn't need any medicine because her baby was coming. Destiny kept begging the nurse for some medicine. The nurse said, I'm getting ready to give you something right now, your baby. The doctor walked in the room and the nurse saw the baby's head and she told Destiny to push. Destiny pushed; the nurse told her to push again. The nurse told her to push one more time and the baby was out. Destiny heard the baby cry and she heard her husband say it's a girl. The nurse told Destiny, we are washing her up, you can see her when we finish. Destiny noticed with her peripheral vision Daniel was taking pictures with the baby. Destiny cleared her throat, "Excuse me can I see my baby?" Destiny laughed to herself that they were doing a photo shoot with her newborn baby!!

When they gave Destiny her baby, she fell in love with her instantly. She had her name immediately Erica Danielle Hardwick. She had the same coloring as Destiny had when she was born, very light. Destiny ended up being a caramel complexion, so Destiny said. "She will get some color like her Mommy did when she gets in the sun." Destiny looked at her eyes and they were blue. Her mother-in-law told her that Daniel's eyes were blue when he was born. She was glad Susan had that talk with her because no one in Destiny's family had blue eyes. Erica had the nerve to have a little hairstyle going on, it was a little Mohawk. Her hair was Sandy brown. Destiny, Carrie and Edmond Sr. had that same hair color. This hair color was passed down from generation of people on Edmond's side of the family. His mother had soft Sandy brown hair. This little lady embodied characteristics already of both sides of the family.

Destiny missed her baby the moment they took her to the nursery. She never knew she could love a person so much. The nurse did finally bring Erica so she could feed her. She said that nothing was wrong with Erica's lungs. Her little voice was rather loud. She was not happy when she was hungry, just like her Mom Destiny. Her roommate had a little boy and he was adorable. She told Destiny her baby was beautiful. Destiny thanked her for the compliment. The two Mom's marveled at their babies. Destiny heard a knock on her hospital door. It was a variety of hospital staff coming to see her baby. They said, "We heard she was a beautiful baby can we see her?" Destiny was a proud Mommy and said of course. When they left her family showed up. Destiny told her mom when Erica was born. She looked just like her. Destiny had never seen her Dad so wrapped up in a baby before. It was love at first sight for everybody. Her sister Carrie said that she was the cutest baby ever.

When her family left Destiny became very ill. The doctor decided to keep her at the hospital because her temperature was 102.3. When her mother came to visit her, she was out of it. She told her mother my temper sounds like a radio station ID. Destiny was defiantly delirious. The doctors wouldn't let Erica breastfeed from Destiny because of the high temperature. Unfortunately, Erica had to drink the baby formula. This would cause an issue later. Since Erica couldn't have her Mother's breast milk it was hard for Destiny to get her to latch on. She would only latch on at night. Destiny's temperature finally broke and she was allowed to go home. She was happy to go home because the food was awful.

While Destiny was still in the hospital Daniel moved them out of the townhouse into the house. Destiny knew a Pastor from her past. Her Mother use to play the organ at his church. His name was Nathan Porter. He and his wife were moving to Atlanta and wanted to sell their house. Pastor Porter told them they could move in immediately. They could do a rent to own until they were ready to buy the house from them. She went back to the townhouse to get a few things then they were gone. She couldn't believe he moved them that quick. The baby had her own bedroom. Destiny wasn't ready for the baby to be by herself, so she put her bassinet in her and Daniel's room. Erica hated for her Dad to touch her Mom or even get in the bed with her. Destiny laughed it off at first, but this baby knew something that her Mom didn't realize about her husband. It would soon come to light.

Daniel secured an excellent job in Orland Park. He worked for an engineering company. He was making about $70,000. Destiny was so excited that Daniel secured such a great job. Destiny found a 3-bedroom house in Homewood. The Hardwick's wanted another child so they needed another bedroom. Destiny had a family that was a Pastor, they were moving to Atlanta. They told them they could move in immediately. They could do a rent to own until they were ready by the house from them. Destiny couldn't believe everything was going so well for them. They told Pastor Porter and his wife Martha that they wanted the house. Destiny called her Mom and told her the good news. Destiny couldn't wait to tell Denise the great news! The house even looked like Marco and Denise's house.

Destiny always waited for the other shoe to drop when things were going too perfect. Daniel started acting erratic once they settled into their condo. Destiny's beloved Aunt Elaine on her Mom's side called and wanted to see Erica. She hadn't seen the baby because right before Erica was born. She became ill. Elaine was a History Teacher at Whitney Young

High School in Chicago and she woke up to get ready for work when she tried to stand up her legs gave out and she fell to the floor. Her oldest son was deceased and her younger son was away at college in Florida. She crawled downstairs and called the ambulance. All the cartilage in both her knees were gone. She needed a double knee replacement, but she needed to lose some weight first. She was obese at the time. She was now confined to a wheelchair. She made it work for her. She still worked at the High School and she also worked as a professor at the College of DuPage. She was finally out of the Hospital and wanted to see Erica.

The day that Destiny was taking Erica to see Aunt Elaine it was below zero. Destiny called her Auntie. Auntie was so excited to see her new baby. Daniel thought it was too cold to take the baby out so in order not to get into an argument she left the baby with Daniel. Courtney and Carrie came to pick Destiny up to go visit Auntie. When they all arrived at Auntie's house. She was so excited to see everybody. She noticed that Erica wasn't with them. Destiny told her what happened. She told her Aunt that one time she was taking

Erica to visit her mother and Daniel called her and told her if she didn't turn around and come back. He was going to throw all of her stuff in the hallway of their condo. She turned around immediately and went back home. As she was telling the story Daniel called her on her cell phone. He told her to come home immediately. She asked him if the baby was alright. He said yes but he missed her and wanted her to come home. She told him that since she came with her Mom and sister. She couldn't leave without them. He said, "Fine if you don't come home now I will take the baby with me to Michigan City and never return back to Chicago to be with you."

Destiny didn't believe Daniel would kidnap their child. She just decided to enjoy her visit with her Aunt. They stayed at her Aunt's house for about 4 hours and then they headed home. When Destiny returned home the condo was dark. Daniel and the baby were gone. She immediately called him to find out where he was. When he answered she asked him why he took the baby out if he thought it was too cold. She was only 2 months old and since it was the evening the temperature had dipped even lower. He told her he was taking the baby to his Ex-girlfriend's home in Michigan City, IN. Destiny didn't even know who he was talking about. She didn't have a address. She was frantic. She started praying and the Holy Spirit directed her to call Denise her sister-in-law. Denise told Destiny that she would call him. Destiny waited for Susan to call her back before she called the police. When Denise called him. He said, I'm never coming back. She said," Daniel I am a Nurse, "Please take her home out of this frigid cold weather." Denise kept talking to him about her being such a little baby and her concern for her health. He finally consented to bring her back home to her mother. When Denise told Destiny, he was on his way home she almost fainted. When he walked through the door, she tackled him. This was the first time he was afraid of Destiny. Daniel had her in her stroller, so Destiny ran over to her baby and grabbed her. Daniel walked past them but then started crying and said, "Denise made me realize how crazy I was being." Destiny had no words for Daniel. She just went into their room with the baby and laid down.

Destiny's Mom was a High School Counselor and Destiny took a lot psychology courses when she was in college because she wanted to be a Mental Health Counselor at some point in her life. After confiding in her Mom and a psychologist Daniel was diagnosed with bi-polar disorder. Which would explain why he often made poor decisions with little regard to the consequences. When she approached Daniel with her findings. He didn't seem surprised. He told her, "I know something is wrong with me." He found a fantastic Psychotherapist. He was getting treatment and things were going so much better.

Destiny found out that Daniel had stopped going to his counseling sessions accidentally. Destiny was asked to join a session she got the date wrong when she showed up the psychologist said he missed his last two appointments because he was ill. Destiny didn't know any of this information. This particular week must have been the week of discovery she also found out he was drinking a lot, doing drugs and gambling. He would go missing from the condo for days. He called her and told her he was okay and was still going to work. Daniel then had the nerve to send his cousin Dennis over to check on her. This man just got out of jail. Dennis actually was a really nice guy. He told Destiny that his cousin was stupid to leave his beautiful wife by herself with a young baby. He told Destiny that he would make sure nothing ever happened to her. Destiny looked at him and said, "You have way more sense than your lunatic cousin." Dennis started laughing and agreed with Destiny.

Destiny went through this with her first husband. Why was history repeating itself again? She wasn't going to put up with his getting high on marijuana, getting drunk, doing cocaine, popping pills, and gambling. Destiny was a Mom now and she didn't want her daughter growing up in dysfunctional family. Destiny couldn't believe that Daniel was the main one that wanted to get married and he wasn't being a good father or a good husband.

Destiny called her Mom and asked her what she should do after all Dad did some of the same things that Daniel was doing except drugs, her Dad never did drugs. Her Mom gave her some sound advice. She suggested going to a Christian Counselor, praying for their marriage and also talking to him about the situation. When Destiny approached Daniel to discuss their marital problems, she couldn't believe what he said. He told her that he was mentally being tortured because she had embarrassed him. Destiny was shocked, this is the first time Destiny heard about his woes. She wandered what she did to embarrass him. He told her he was talking to his Mom and she said Erica didn't look anything like him or their family. Destiny could always recognize a satanic attack. She knew that her marriage was being attacked. She decided to fight for her marriage. She started praying and the Holy Spirit let her know that this was defiantly an attack on her marriage.

The Devil uses people and his mother was being used by the devil. Daniel had previously disclosed to Destiny that his mother is always starting mayhem. Susan had tried on numerous occasions to destroy Marco and Denise's marriage. They had separated a couple of times, but they always found their way back to each other. Destiny remembered the Bible verse: Proverbs 6:18-19: A heart that devises wicked plans, Feet that are swift in running to evil, A false witness who speaks lies, and one who sows discord among the brethren. Destiny recognized Susan's divisive behavior. She was speaking lies about Destiny because of the things in her own life. Destiny wasn't a cheater. She didn't marry Daniel and then conceive a baby by another man, which is what his mother did when Daniel's Dad was in jail.

Destiny asked Daniel why he started believing Erica wasn't his biological child. He said she is just so light. She isn't the same color as my son and my son looks just like me. Destiny looked at him and said," Are you kidding me?" "You sound really ignorant and uneducated!" He replied, "How dare you insult me like that!" Destiny apologized but she stated, "How long have African American been going through the whole skin complexion debate?" Daniel just kept talking about how light she was. Destiny told him that she was lighter than everyone in her immediate family, and they are her family. He said, but you got a little darker Erica is light bright damn near white. Destiny said, "Let me stop talking to you because you sound crazy as hell." Destiny said, her own mother was wandering why she was so light, but Edmond reminded Courtney his mother was extremely light. Daniel just looked at Destiny like she was lying when she told him about her family background. Her Dad teased his wife about Destiny's skin color, but he never disputed the fact that he was her Dad. Daniel said, "Can we get a DNA test to prove she is my daughter." Destiny said, "You are within your rights to do whatever you want to do. I can't stop you."

Daniel asked Destiny to bring Erica to Trinity Hospital in Chicago for the DNA test. The nurse laughed at him and said, "Anyone can plainly see she looks like you and your wife." Destiny laughed and said, "Tell that to his meddling Mom." Destiny was boiling inside but she wanted to keep her family together." Daniel didn't tell her that the test was $750. She found out because he received a bill in the mail. They wouldn't give us the results until he paid the bill. When Destiny approached him about the whole situation. He threatened to hurt her if she didn't pay for the test. When she stood up to him. He said he would put her out.

Daniel blamed all his emotional problems on the whole baby gate situation. She was holding their 3-month-old daughter and he pushed her and knocked her down. She was dazed and confused. She couldn't believe he not only pushed her, but he could have hurt their infant daughter. She realized what type of person she was married to. He was a monster in her eyes. She immediately packed her and the baby's things up and left the condo. Her parents and sister were visiting her brother in Carson, California. She had her parents' house to herself along with the baby. Her parents were gone for a week. Destiny needed time away from her husband. She was hoping that her disappearance from the family home would make him miss her and he would get himself together for the sake of their family.

When her parents returned and when they found Destiny there. They wondered what was going on. Destiny didn't dare tell her Dad the real story because her Dad could be a thug. He had slowed down a lot, but he still was crazy. He had many contacts he could call, and Daniel would get a bloody beat down. Her brother was crazy as well. He was a naval officer and she didn't want any problems. The next day the doorbell rang. It was Daniel. Destiny heard him say "Is my family here?" Her Dad said, "Yes come on in they are here. She heard them talking and Daniel was being extra phony saying he missed them. He was here to take Destiny home. Destiny had driven herself there she didn't need him to come get her. She decided she would try to work things out with Daniel because of Erica. She didn't want her to grow up without her father. When Destiny appeared, Daniel ran over to her and started crying, hugging her and apologizing for what he did. Her Dad couldn't hear what he was saying he was so impressed that Daniel came to get his family. Her Dad still thought it was a little argument and that Destiny had forgiven him He had no idea how violent Daniel was to his daughter and granddaughter.

When the Hardwick's returned home Daniel was the perfect husband, which lasted about 2 weeks. She came home one day. He asked her for some money. She didn't know he was still spending his money on drugs. Destiny told him no and she left the house. When Destiny left Daniel started ransacking the house looking for money. She found everything in the closet on the floor and on the bed. When she started cleaning up everything, she noticed pictures of her Ex-Fiancé Steve on the bed. When he came home. He accused Destiny of sleeping with Steve and he was Erica's father. Destiny couldn't believe that just because Erica was fair that she was Steve's child. Daniel pointed out not only was Erica light but she had curly hair and her eyes changed colors like Steve. Steve had grey eyes, but they didn't change colors. He viciously attacked her and dragged her over to the window. Destiny was screaming, they were lived on the 11th floor she realized he was trying to throw her out of the window. Destiny kicked him in his groan, and he released his grip on her. She started praying and the Holy Spirit told her what to say to Daniel. She said, I will call him and you can talk to him." He stopped in his tracks and said, "Call him now!!!" Destiny made sure that the speaker was on so Daniel could hear the conversation. When Destiny dialed the number Steve's mother answered the phone. She recognized Destiny's voice right away. She was such a nice Christian woman and she was so excited to hear Destiny's voice. Daniel went into a frenzy,

"Why are you talking to his Mom shut the hell up talking to her and ask for her son!" He slapped across her face and she flew into the kitchen table. He picked her up like a rag doll and slapped her again with so much force she went flying across the room again and back into the kitchen table and chairs. Destiny was screaming and in so much pain. Steve's mother heard everything. She asks if Destiny was okay. When she got up off the floor, she told her she was fine. Steve's Mom said that he wasn't there. Destiny left her number and then she hung up.

Destiny knew she couldn't keep living like this, she started making plans to leave Daniel. Daniel was always apologetic when he had one of his abusive outburst. Carrie called Destiny and said she had a dream that Daniel had killed multiple people and put them in her garage. Destiny didn't take the dream literally that her sister had but she felt that it did have a meaning and the meaning was that if she didn't escape from this marriage. He would kill her.

CHAPTER 8

Destiny On Her Own Again

————·•·•·——

Destiny had two bright spots in her life. Her daughter and her job. She was riding in the car with two of her colleagues Cathy and Jackie, when her phone rang. It was Daniel. Destiny was just basically co-existing with her husband. He told her he wanted her out of the condo unless she paid the $750 for the DNA test. Destiny told him once again why she would pay for test to tell her something she already knew. It was impossible for Erica to be anyone else's baby. Destiny wasn't very sexually active when she was single because she was really trying to live by the Bible and not fornicate. She never cheated on Daniel, so it was impossible for Erica to be any other man's child. Destiny said, "Fine I will move out. She went to pick up Erica from the babysitter's house.

When she arrived home to pack up her stuff Daniel looked like he was high as a kite. He didn't go to work and had been getting high all day. She just ignored him and kept packing up her stuff. Courtney arrived to help her. She started packing Erica's clothes. All of a sudden Daniel jumped up and said, "Hurry up". Courtney said, we are going as fast as we can. Daniel didn't like what Courtney said to him. He said, "You're not going fast enough. "The next thing Destiny knew he savagely attacked her. He started pulling her hair, slapping and then punching her. Her Mother ran to make sure the Baby was okay. Eric was in her carrier on the bed. Destiny told her Mother to call the police. When she was calling the police, Destiny started fighting him back. Whenever you are fighting a Demon. They have superhuman strength. He threw Destiny to the ground and jumped on her and started to strangle her. Her Mom was trying to pull him off. When he turned around Destiny hit him in the head with the baby's bassinet. He was dazed and confusion began to set in, that's when Destiny said, "Mom we need to go." They ran out of the door.

When they arrived downstairs, the police were outside. Her Mom told Destiny to go out and direct the police where to go. Destiny didn't realize that she was all bruised up until the police officers looked at her and asked her if she was okay. Destiny will never forget the look of horror on the police officers face. This situation triggered an adrenaline rush she didn't even realize how bad she was bruised up. The next thing Destiny knew she was on the ground, she had fainted. She didn't want to go to the hospital. Daniel ran and the police didn't catch him. Destiny pressed charges against him for Domestic Battery. Destiny and her Mom asked for an order of protection against Daniel. Destiny felt the Order of Protection would help her keep Daniel away from her. He couldn't contact her via telephone calls, mail, email, written notes, or third parties. He was supposed to stay away from her job and home. Daniel of course did all of the above like the order didn't exist. He was finally caught and spent days in jail for violating the Order of Protection. He kept begging Destiny to take him back. Destiny knew this man was truly crazy. Her friend Cathy said that Daniel had come to her house to talk to her. When she opened the door he said, please tell your friend

Destiny to call her goons off of me. Destiny had no idea what she was talking about. Destiny didn't send anyone to beat Daniel up.

Destiny was talking to her Mom about what Cathy said, her mother ended up telling her that her Dad had reached out to her Ex-Fiancé and hired him to protect her. He paid Steve $700 to handle Daniel. Destiny felt bad at first when she heard this information. She started feeling less guilty when she found out some of the things Daniel was doing. For example: He came to Carrie's house looking for Destiny and Erica even though there was an order of protection against him. He still stalked Destiny every chance he got. Her father wasn't going to keep putting up with this man shenanigans. Destiny reached out to Steve to ask him for more information on what her Dad hired him to do. Steve told her everything she wanted to know. He said, Edmond hired him and two other guys. They beat Daniel up and put a gun in his mouth." Steve said they told him never to bother you again. They then let him go and he ran away as fast as his feet would carry him. Steve said, he was happy that Edmond Sr. contacted him regarding beating up Daniel. Steve was sad about Destiny being in an abusive relationship. He felt that if he had not been such a deadbeat she would not have left and ran into the arms of Daniel. Steve's mother told him she heard Daniel attacking her the day that she called to speak with Steve. Destiny told Steve that she called him so he could verify that Erica was not his child. Steve, shouted, "What? How could she be my child we were over for a year?" Destiny agreed with him and she was trying to convince Daniel Erica wasn't Steve's child. Steve replied, " Daniel was really a lunatic, wasn't he? Destiny responded, "Yes he was and so was his Mom."

Destiny was friends with a young lady who use to babysit her daughter. She helped Destiny file for her divorce without an attorney. It was a lot of work, but Destiny didn't want to borrow money from anyone. Destiny hated that she had to take her 6-month-old baby away from her Dad, but he was dangerous. He had already tried to kidnap her once before. She just didn't trust him. The divorce took about 10 months. Destiny had moved in with her parents because she felt she would be safe. Destiny had the most supportive family and friends if it had not been for her support system. She would have had a nervous breakdown. She realized that her relationship with God was also a blessing. Destiny knew she could have been hurt badly or killed. Destiny had to get out of her parents' house her Dad was cool, but her Mom was treating her like a child. Destiny moved back into her old townhouse when she thought it was safe.

Destiny had a very good job. She was glad that her baby wouldn't have to suffer because now Destiny was a single parent. She received a promotion and a raise. Once again, her life was getting better but her personal life sucked. She kept herself busy and the only thing that was really important to her was raising Erica. She didn't date a lot because she didn't trust many men, especially around her daughter.

Destiny enjoyed singing in her church choir and in another professional choir that often appeared on television, competed in talent contests and traveled. Her performing in the choir kept her really busy. The choir had a concert every year. She enjoyed her church very much. Her sister had gotten licensed 2 years ago. Destiny knew God was calling her to the ministry, but she tried to run. When God saved her from being thrown from a 11th story window and a vicious beat down from her ex-husband she knew it was time to answer the call into ministry. Her church home God's Glory Non-Denominational Church had classes for a year that met every Saturday. When the New Year came Destiny was a licensed Minister. Destiny always credited her Mom for being her first Sunday School Teacher. She started reading bible stories to her at the age of 4 years old. Her love for God grew every day of her life.

Erica was getting love from Destiny's family. Daniel's family turned on Erica and Destiny. They claimed Erica wasn't his child. Destiny felt sorry for his family and prayed that they would have a relationship with God one day. His family abandoned Erica. The only person Destiny spoke to in his family was Mario's wife Denise. They hadn't spoken to her in years but whenever they did, they acted like no time had passed between then.

Destiny decided that a new year would bring a new love. A lady she met when she was doing extra work had befriended her. She was about 15 years older than Destiny and her name was Betty. Betty had a prophetic gift. She told Destiny that she would get married before Erica turned 5 years old. This word was being confirmed because Destiny's cousin told her she would be getting married soon. Her daughter Erica was 3 years old at this time. Destiny was just happy that she had a full life and that she wasn't going to put up with any more abuse.

Destiny's old roommate Gerri talked her into online dating. She had used the personals in the newspaper so online dating shouldn't be that different Destiny thought to herself. The first guy was a disaster. He was left at the altar when he was getting married, if that wasn't enough the woman who left him for another man found her husband in bed with another man. She tried to come back to the guy I was talking too. I told him this is too much and I didn't talk to him again. The next guy seemed really nice his name was Richard. They were messaging each other one day and he asked her for her email address. They started emailing each other back and forth and then he asked her for her phone number. When they started talking on the phone, they realized they had grown up together and he use to hang out with her brother. Her brother even had a crush on his older sister. His sister was 3 years older than her brother and she never paid attention to her brother's friends. Their first conversation lasted 2 hours. Destiny had never been on the phone with someone for that long. She was totally liking this new guy.

She let Richard know that she would be going to a conference with her job. They decided to meet at the hotel where the conference was being held. Her meetings usually ended early. She knew they could spend the rest of the evening together. When she reached the conference the organizers of the conference were acting funny. The next day Destiny was laid off and sent home in a limousine. She was devastated because she loved that job. Destiny did realize that God had something better for her and that is always a blessing. Destiny was nervous about telling her new friend Richard about getting laid off. She called him and told him she was no longer at the conference because she got laid off. He was so understanding. The very next day he came over with candles, a foot bath and soft music to make her feel better. Destiny knew that was a straight player move but she still felt it was thoughtful. Richard was really great and understanding. Destiny prayed about getting someone totally different from any man she had ever been with and that was Richard!

Richard and Destiny were inseparable from the first time they talked. He worked for Chicago Board of Education. He would have to travel to Springfield, IL for his job sometimes to take care of business. He hated going there. They were dating for about 3 months and he called her and told her he missed her and that he was in love with her. Destiny had no idea he felt this way, but she felt he was being genuine. When Richard returned to Chicago. He called Destiny, he said he wanted to discuss something with her. When Richard arrived at Destiny's house, he told her he wanted to introduce her to his Mom. Destiny was nervous this was a big step in a relationship when a guy starts introducing you to his family.

When they arrive at Richard's house his Mom Leah Cage didn't know Destiny was coming. She was in her robe and slippers. It was on a Sunday evening and she was relaxing. She was really sweet about me coming over to visit. Richard owned a apartment building in Broadview, IL. Which is a Western Suburb in Illinois. He rented out all the units. He didn't live there because his father had recently passed away and he was there helping his parents. Richard was such as thoughtful guy he stayed there to make sure his Mom was okay. He told Destiny he was ready to move out now that he knew his Mom was okay without his Dad. He only had a sister named Regina in which Destiny met 2 weeks after meeting Mrs. Cage.

Destiny had been seeing Richard for 5 months now and she started falling in love with him. She didn't need any financial help, but Richard told her he would be happy to help her with any help she needed. Destiny received a nice financial package when she got laid off. She received her same pay every two weeks. She was also receiving unemployment. She even had medical insurance for her and Erica. She would lose her medical Insurance in a month. She knew that she would need to secure another job for medical insurance.

Destiny and Richard were celebrating their 6-month anniversary. He asked her to go to the Mall with him because he wanted to pick something's up before they went out to dinner for their anniversary. She said sure, when they were walking past Whitehall Jewelry Store, he asked her to step into the store. She was thinking he was getting her some earrings for her birthday that was a few days away. He told her to pick out a ring she would like if she was getting married. When she picked out the ring Richard asked her to try it on. She loved the princess cut 3 carat ring it was beautiful. When she put the ring on her finger he got down on his knees and asked her to marry him. Everyone in the store started clapping and of course she said yes!

Destiny usually didn't like surprises, but she loved this surprise. This was the best birthday present ever. Destiny told Richard, "I thought you were getting me my diamond earrings, but I'll accept my surprise proposal. Richard had called their mutual friend David and got his advice. David was a Pastor and one of Richards's really good friends. Richard was a Mason and in the Alpha Phi Alpha Fraternity.

He told Richard that he may have to step back from participating in Mason activates to cultivate his marriage. Destiny was glad she was marrying a guy that was part of the Divine 9 Greek letter organizations. She wouldn't have to explain a lot of things to him. She wanted to marry a guy that was like minded.

Destiny never wanted to put anybody down but the differences she had with her Ex-husbands boiled down to the fact that they weren't on the same page spiritually, financially and educationally. Richard checked all of those boxes. Destiny was raised to not look down on anybody. Carrie called it false guilt because Destiny felt that she was looking down on men when she didn't want to date men that had too many children, uneducated, no car, on drugs, alcoholic, and not financially stable. She felt like they weren't ready for a relationship with her or what she had to offer them. Her sister let her know it's nothing wrong with having standards. The bible says that people should be equally yoked. The person who is usually unstable will bring the stable person down. In Destiny's case that is what was happening to her. Her first and second husbands were dragging her down with all of their various issues.

Destiny would tell anyone who would listen that her daughter was her life. Destiny became more responsible when Erica was born. She would have given her life for her child. She realized she needed to be serious about not allowing any random man to come into her life especially since she was now a Mom. After she divorced Erica's Dad, she rarely let Erica meet men that she was dating. She really prayed about allowing Richard to meet Erica. When Destiny felt it was safe. She introduced Erica to Richard. They instantly bonded and Destiny could tell her 4-year-old daughter liked him. Erica was a very inquisitive child and after about a month she said," Mr. Cage can I call you Daddy Rich?" He said of course Erica. One day Erica asked Destiny. "Why doesn't Daddy Rich live with us?" Destiny said, "He doesn't live here because we aren't married yet." Erica said, oh okay," Destiny's explanation was good enough for her. Then she ran off to play outside.

Erica always wanted sisters and brothers to play with outside, play board games with and watch television with. She had a half-brother, but she was never around him. Richard had a 15-year-old son from a woman he dated briefly and an 8-year-old daughter from his first wife. He didn't have any children from his second wife. When Erica met her soon to be stepsister and brother, she liked them as much as she liked their Dad. Destiny would have never entertained marrying Rich, as she called him if her daughter didn't like him or the children. Destiny knew that she already had to fight against her prior emotions from two other marriages she didn't want her daughter to be in any type of drama period!

Destiny wanted to get married in June, because her first one was in July and the second one was in February. Richard agreed to their date of June 10th. They had a whole year to plan their perfect wedding. She first wanted a wedding with guests but as time ticked on. She wanted a very small wedding with immediate family only. They were going to have a small wedding reception with about 100 people. Destiny was going to pay for the reception, everything she was wearing; dress, shoes, jewelry, etc. her mother was paying for the flowers, Rich was paying for the honeymoon. Destiny was still living in her old townhouse with her sister Carrie. Rich knew they needed to move into a house. They started looking for a house about 3 months before they were to marry. Rich told her she could have whatever house she wanted as long as it was in his budget. He gave her the amount for the house which was that she could spend under $190,000.00. Destiny was off and running to find her new home. She narrowed it down to two houses. One was in Homewood, IL and the other one was in Country Club Hills, IL. They looked at both and liked both but the house in Homewood, IL was a little bit more expensive than the home in Country Club Hills, IL. They chose the one in Country Club Hills, IL.

Rich was so romantic. He would write poems and love notes to Destiny every other month until the day they walked down the aisle. He would tell her till death would they part, flowers and dirt he would say were the only thing that would separate them. She felt the same way. She was elated she finally found her soul mate. His relationship with God was great as well. The wedding was around the corner. Destiny couldn't believe a year was almost here. She was getting nervous as her wedding day approached. Destiny couldn't believe that she would be married for a third time. She knew the first 2 were huge mistakes. She didn't want to have a baby out of wedlock. She realized this time she wasn't in a hurry to just be with someone this was real love unlike her other two marriages. Destiny and Rich would say, "You're my forever, my real spouse, the other ones were phony." She thought that they would grow old and grey together.

CHAPTER 9

Dreams Shattered

----··•••··----

The wedding did have a few hiccups. Destiny was wandering why Richard and his son were late. His son Brian left his dress shoes at home, so he had to wear gym shoes to the wedding. Destiny was fine with them being a little late as long as the love of her life had arrived. The ceremony was short but beautiful. Destiny had made Richard wait for sex while they were dating so Richard said he couldn't sit through a reception without thinking about sex. When they were driving to the reception, they took a detour to her old townhouse and made love. The marriage was officially consummated!

The reception was nice and simple. A young lady named Karen coordinated the reception. Carrie sang a song for the Bride and Groom. Destiny and Rich wanted a small celebration because they had both been married 2 times, wanted to buy a house and were traveling to Jamaica for the honeymoon. The happy couple left their reception and stayed in a hotel before they left for the honeymoon spot. His daughter loved her parents so much that she stayed with them along with Erica. Erica acted a lot like Rich they were born in the same month, November. Rich's daughter Mia was a lot like Destiny because growing up Destiny was a very picky eater and so was Mia. Courtney told Mia to write down everything she liked on a piece of paper. The list was short it was only 10 things on the list. Mia loved bacon, one morning Courtney asked Mia want she wanted for breakfast. She said 4 biscuits and 6 pieces of bacon. Courtney was shocked, she said" I can give you 3 pieces of bacon and 2 biscuits." My husband doesn't even eat 6 pieces of bacon!!

Destiny and Rich were gone for 5 days and they enjoyed themselves immensely. When they arrived back home, they were ready to start their new life together. Rich presented Destiny with her own credit card with a $4,000 limit. She had never even had a card with a limit over $500. She was elated but she promised Rich she would only use it for emergencies.

The next couple of years were great. They moved into their new home a month after being married. This is the happiest Destiny had ever been. The only thing that topped this marriage was the birth of Erica. Destiny was truly in love and thank God for blessing her life finally.

Destiny started to notice something's about Rich's personality about 2 months after they got married but it didn't bother her, it just let her know he wasn't perfect. Christmas was her favorite holiday. Rich hated Christmas and was almost a Scrooge. He didn't even want Destiny to put up a Christmas tree. Destiny asked Rich why he hated Christmas. He said it had something to do with his childhood. His Dad would go on a trip every year after Thanksgiving right before Christmas and it never mattered if the family could afford it or not. Destiny believed that whatever happened it wasn't bad enough to hold onto it forever. Her parents made many mistakes, but she forgave them. When you don't forgive others bitterness festers like an open wound, which means your wound never heals. She would soon see that he had an unforgiving spirit that would soon extend to her as well.

Destiny said, "We can't make the children suffer because of your issues." She demanded he get them a tree or she would go get the tree from her sister's house given to her from her ex-fiancée Steve. Destiny knew when those words flew out of her mouth that it was mean. What she did was one of the worse things you can do to a man is throw up something another man did for you. She felt bad but it worked Rich said they could stop by the store and pick up a tree after bible study.

Rich decided to pay all the bills in the house except for the water bill. Destiny was elated that he took on that responsibility. When she was working, she did contribute what could to the household expenses. Destiny and Rich were both a little spoiled. Destiny enjoyed getting her way and so did Rich. Destiny didn't want to be selfish and would just let Rich have his way a lot of times. Rich would do a lot of things behind Destiny's back. He would preach about them being a team but turn around and make decisions regarding the house without her knowledge. One example of this is when they first moved into their home. She woke up one morning to men in her house putting in an Alarm system. Destiny said, "When did you decide to get an alarm system?" Rich said," The house didn't look safe, so I decided to get the alarm system." It wasn't that Destiny disagreed with him, but he never even discussed it with her. He started to be really controlling on important decisions that a married couple should make together. Destiny was very irritated by him being controlling but it still never stopped her from loving him. Destiny began to see that Rich thought she was a damsel in distress and that she should be happy that he saved her from her miserable life. He thought she was down and out. She might have been down, but she would never be out. Her life might not have been perfect, but it wasn't miserable.

Destiny was a licensed Minister and she knew that Rich had a ministerial call on his life. Rich had been running from his Ministerial calling for years. He finally accepted his calling and they were both ordained October 2007. Destiny was so excited that they both were being obedient to God's call. Cassie told Destiny that within the next 6 months that they would be over a church. Destiny usually believed Cassie, but she thought this was a little farfetched. Destiny had to apologize to Carrie because they ended up taking the reins over from his friend David. David was asked to step down as Pastor because while serving as Pastor of his church he impregnated a woman he was having an affair with.

David kept asking about the church instead of getting himself together. Rich and Destiny went on vacation and David stepped in to preach while they were gone. He took back the church. Rich and Destiny started a Bible Study out of their home for 1 year. They started looking for a place to have their services. Destiny's Aunt Emma helped them secure a place for their church to worship at a Huge church Called Bethany. Aunt Emma died a year later. She had cancer and she wanted Rich and Destiny to get settled into their church home before she made her transition.

Destiny and Rich went through a lot of tragedies beginning in 2007 to 2013 Destiny lost about 12 family members. Destiny was devastated over all of these deaths. She lost Aunts, Uncles and cousins. The worst of all was the death of her beloved Father in 2008. Her Dad had been sick. He had quadruple bypass surgery in 2007. He was in pain but even his doctor was surprised he passed away of a massive heart attack. Destiny's had a cousin named Rose that was the same age as her. She passed away in 2009. She had comforted her when her Dad passed away. Destiny became severely depressed. She couldn't eat and when she did eat her stomach hurt more and she had diarrhea. The doctor couldn't find a medical reason and asked Destiny was she under stress. Destiny said she was. The doctor gave her some medicine and it did help. She still had a hard time getting out of the bed because she had become so depressed. She started praying and as usual God responded to her woes. The Holy Spirit begin ministering to her spirit and reminding her that her daughter needed her. Erica was still young. She was only 9 years old and she needed her mother. Destiny realized her daughter didn't ask to be here in fact Destiny remember praying to have a baby. She decided her daughter was more important to her than the depression that was trying to overtake her life. She sought help from her brothers Pastor's wife. She was back feeling great and ready to continue leading her life in a mentally healthy way. She praised God that she overcame depression.

Ed's wife Tina became ill in 2011. She was diagnosed with Stage 4 Cervical Cancer. She fought really hard for 2 years. She passed away August of 2013. Tina and Ed Jr. had 4 children. Destiny took her death really hard. She had known Tina for 27 years. She just couldn't imagine her Sister-in-law not being here with her. Their oldest child Anita was born in July of 1998 and Erica came in November of 1998. Tina would send Erica a whole wardrobe sometimes. She was so nice to Erica. Erica was devastated by the loss of her Aunt. Rich lost a few relatives as well. One of his uncles who was Destiny favorite passed away during this time.

Rich and Destiny enjoyed some high Moments in Ministry. They married several couples, prophesied over people and even given the gift of healing. Destiny's friend was living with her Mom and she felt her Mom's house was hunted. She would see objects move, she and her son were both sick when they were staying there. She called the couple late one night and they started praying for her. Destiny told her to move out immediately. She felt better instantly. She met the young lady at another friend's house in order to pray for her 5-year-old son who was healthy and now couldn't walk and was very ill. Destiny prayed for him. A couple of days later the young lady called Destiny and told her that her son was diagnosed with a brain tumor. She then told her that her son just started walking one day. When she took him back to the doctor, they couldn't find anything wrong with him. A miracle performed by God!!

The membership at the church had started to dwindle. They decided to close the church after being open for 8 years. It was very emotional, but they prayed about it and that was what the Lord told them to do. They not only endured deaths but their jobs were in jeopardy as well. Rich was laid off his six-figure job of 18 years in 2006. Destiny knew she would see a change in him. Destiny started seeing a downward spiral in his life and their marriage. Destiny saw the devil destroying her marriage. She believed the Rich lost his faith. She was in a one woman battle because he dropped out of the battle and gave up on the marriage. Destiny knew you can't fight by yourself. Destiny did everything she could to save their marriage. She thought counseling would help. Rich even told her that he wanted the marriage to work. He lied and went behind her back started planning the demise of their marriage. He was no longer in a relationship with God. Destiny admitted she tried to control some things that Rich did in order to save their marriage. When she would see Rich take a drink, she would chastise him. She just didn't want him to turn into an alcoholic like her Dad. Alcoholism killed her Dad and she didn't want that for her husband. She couldn't believe that 18 years of marriage was going down the drain.

Her Mothers only surviving sister became ill and Destiny and Rich visited her in the hospital. When they arrived home, Rich was acting funny. He came in their bedroom and told her he was unhappy and he was leaving her. He wanted a divorce. Destiny was devastated, but Rich just walked out the door like nothing just happened. Destiny thought wow one day you're married and the next day it's over. She would have never believed that he would walk out on her especially with her Aunt being sick. This was the most heartless and evil act a person could have done to her. He left her to pay all the bills in the house. He told her. I've left so when are you leaving the house? She was trying to figure out why he wanted her to leave especially since he was gone and he vowed never to come back to her or the house. Destiny didn't even recognize this person in front of her. This isn't the man she fell in love with and married. Destiny just looked at him and said nothing. The next day she woke up and thought to herself that she should call her mother so she could move in with her. Then she heard the Holy Spirit say, "No one told you to move." Destiny was shocked but she decided to be obedient to the Holy Spirit. She decided she would stay in the house.

Destiny prayed and asked God why would he allow her to marry Rich? This man did things in secret to plan her demise. She realized they had radically different views on money and giving. God answered her and said, "You just answered your own question." Iron sharpens Iron, Rich had some skills you needed and you had some he needed. Destiny was giving, he was selfish. God put him with a woman who lost her job. He started changing his attitude because of his love for her. That's when Satan stepped in and said, "Why are you giving this woman anything?" He told Rich, "Destiny was using him." Rich stopped listening to God's voice and started listening to Satan's lies. Satan's plans will destroy what God has put together.

Destiny's testimony is that people are not God. You can't worship people because they will let you down. She knew that since she was single again, that she would be responsible for her daughter and herself. Destiny had men that told her they would take care of her every need. Destiny might have been born at 2am but she wasn't born yesterday morning. She knew she would have to do something to get that money. She was angry that men were trying to use her in her time of need. She had a conversation with God that she wouldn't prostitute herself out to pay her bills if God would help her out. God promised Destiny that he would make sure Destiny could stay in her home. Destiny actually saw several miracles that unfolded in front of her on a monthly basis. She was never behind on any bills and she had money to spare and buy things she wanted. When she was married, they were behind on their bills sometimes. God took care of her needs and wants better than her husband did! One of her miracles was a check she received for $800 as part of a settlement. She never received that much money on a mass settlement that other consumers were involved in. When she received settlements in the past it may be $25 at the most.

When Destiny started her healing process, she started thinking how long he had planned his departure. He had been planning on leaving for about 2 years. He had talked to his mother about it and she told him to do whatever made him happy. Destiny was shocked when she heard those words come out of his Mom's mouth. She didn't take up for Destiny at all. How heartless can a person be, she felt betrayed! Destiny noticed that his Mother-in-law stopped supporting Erica. She stopped coming to any of Erica's functions the year she was graduating from High School. Her mother-in-law had washed her hands of Erica and Destiny. This was a conspiracy done by two people she thought loved her. She was devastated by their deceit. The divorce took about a year. She was divorced in September and her Aunt passed away in

November on Thanksgiving Day. Her Aunt's two sons were deceased, so she left money and part of her Condominium to Destiny. She also made Destiny the Executor of her Estate.

Destiny was numb. She was talking to her lawyer and he said he heard that the three most stressful things to happen to people are: death, moving to another place and divorce. Destiny had endured all three. The support of her friends and family was phenomenal. Destiny believed that you can't keep a good woman down. Destiny became instantly wealthy after feeling like she couldn't make it from day to day. She was sitting at her house and the Holy Spirit told her it was now time to move. She was trying to decide if she should purchase her house but there were too many painful memories in that home. She felt she wouldn't heal properly staying in that home. She was looking at a real estate page and a beautiful house popped up. It was around the corner from her mother. She knew she couldn't afford to live in that area, but God reminded her that she was in another financial bracket now thanks to her Aunts generosity. The house also was going for a reduced price because the family wanted a quick sell. When she walked in all she saw was a sea of pink. The house had pink carpets, lighting fixtures and tile in the bathrooms. She was in love. She knew this was her house. The Realtor said another lady wanted to see the house, but she kept moving the days back to see the house. They decided to accept Destiny's offer.

Destiny was elated that she was moving into an upper middle-class neighborhood and that she was getting the house of her dreams. Her old house was nice, but this house was even nicer. Destiny downsized a little. Her old house was three levels, 2400 square feet, with 4 bedrooms, and 3 bathrooms. Her new house was 1900 square feet 3 bedrooms, 3 bathrooms but was a ranch with a basement. Destiny still wanted space and she was very happy with her choice. Destiny was still dealing with the death of mother's last sibling. She was very close to her Aunt. Her Aunt Elaine loaned her $3,000 to get her divorce from Rich. Elaine really loved Rich, but when she found out how horrible he treated Destiny for no good reason she was really upset with him as well as the rest of Destiny's family.

Destiny also had to sell Auntie's Condo. Her Aunt was the Shopping Home Network Queen. She ordered from there every chance she got. She would turn on her television and check to see if there was anything she could order. She was addicted to shopping. She also loved shopping online. Destiny decided to sell her Aunt's Condo. She started going through her things and she found out she had so much stuff she decided to have an Estate sale to sell her things to other people. Destiny made almost $3,000 on her stuff but spent $1,000 because she had to have people get rid of things she couldn't sell and didn't need. She pawned stuff off on people until everything was gone.

Destiny was now ready to close on her new home and sell her Aunts place. She had the closing for her house in March on a Tuesday and the a few days later on Friday was the closing for her Aunts home. Destiny was exhausted she knew she was running from her feelings about her divorce and her Aunts death. She knew that she needed something to keep her busy. Destiny wanted to heal which meant mediating on what went wrong something she really didn't do when she broke up with her prior husbands. She waited a while to date and even when she did date none of the guys lived in Illinois. She knew she wasn't ready for a relationship. She just wanted to have male companionship, good conversations, and go out from time to time when they came to visit her from out of town.

Rich had no idea that Destiny had moved out of their home. She wanted to make sure that she had moved into the new house before she told him. He never liked Destiny telling him something and then it didn't work out. He would blame her no matter if it was her fault or not. She would have flashback of times that an employer didn't pay her. He would be so mad it felt like he blamed Destiny for the job failing to pay. Rich hit the roof when he found out she moved. He said, "No one lives there now?" Destiny told him No!! Destiny had mentioned to him that she was trying to rent the house but didn't have any luck. The house was now vacant. Destiny suggested Rich move back in and several months later he ended up moving back into the house.

Rich had never really lost contact with Destiny. He wanted to be friends with Destiny, but she was too hurt to even consider a friendship with him. She told him he was dead to her, called his mother a liar and snapped at him every chance she got. She later apologized for her temper tantrums and talking about his mother. Destiny felt like if she treated him nice and forgave him then she was letting him off the hook for mistreating, abandoning and treating her like a piece of crap under his shoe. She knew better then to have an unforgiving spirit. She knew deep down inside that she couldn't keep hating his guts. She knew she had to forgive him and his mother. She truly wanted to heal, but true healing would only come with true forgiveness. She wanted to be better not bitter and she was becoming bitter.

She noticed after each one of her divorces she would just move on. She couldn't move on for some reason. She realized what was really eating at her. She felt Rich didn't love her as much as he proclaimed if he did how could he just abandon her. She felt he was deceitful from day one. Rich called her one day and admitted that he tries to be everything to the women in his life to make them happy. She instantly felt sorry for him. He knew that he was weird and didn't think a woman would accept his personality. It was a really nice talk. Destiny told him to never stop being true to himself. She also told him, "If the person is into you and loves you, she will likely accept you for who you are and not who they want you to be. The weird thing about the conversation she was having with her ex-husband is a conversation she should have had with herself. She ignored red flags because she wanted her relationships to work. She wasn't being true to herself and her feelings. She knew that from now on she would need to be patient with the process of getting to know her next relationship. He did tell her that he really did love her. She started to believe that he loved her but had some internal issues he needed to handle.

Destiny felt that all her life people didn't appreciate her and what she had to bring to the table. She was having a conversation with her sister Carrie and she told her "You are your own worst enemy Destiny, if people don't appreciate your worth that's their issue not yours." Destiny instantly realized that Carrie was right. She was the child of the most high God. She realized her worth and she acknowledge that she will no longer let people take her for granted.

Destiny is no longer looking for love. Destiny is allowing love to find her after all, according to Proverbs 18:22 "He that finds a wife finds a good thing and obtains favor from the Lord." Destiny finally realized that her happiness wasn't tied to being with a man. She finally has found peace now with her life and didn't care if she ever got married again. Her priorities were concentrating on her daughter and making sure she was going to graduate from college. She was so proud of Erica because she has been on the honor roll at DePaul University for 4 years. She wants to be there for Erica to support her and her dreams. Destiny remembers her daughters first heart break with her first real boyfriend. She knew she couldn't take her pain away, but she really wanted to just be there for whatever she needed. A lot of times people just want to talk about what they are going through. They may only want someone to listen to them. They may or may not want your advice.

Destiny has 2 businesses. She runs a record label that her Dad started and a PR company. She works from home and she loves her life. She still preaches, teaches and is a mentor to many young girls and women. She learned a lot of valuable lessons from the people God put in her life. She felt like she had to be perfect for people to like her. She realized that she just had to be the best person she could be. She remembered her Mom asking her when she was in school did, she do her best with her schoolwork and when she took her test. She would answer yes. Her Mother would then tell her than if you have done your best then there is nothing else you could have done. She is now living her best life and hoping her daughter, friends and family are also living theirs!

THE END

www.ingramcontent.com/pod-product-compliance
Lightning Source LLC
Chambersburg PA
CBHW050658290626
47170CB00015B/1636